Alex Ryan, Stop That!

Alex Ryan, Stop That!

CLAUDIA MILLS

FARRAR, STRAUS AND GIROUX / NEW YORK

Library of Congress Cataloging-in-Publication Data
Mills, Claudia.
    Alex Ryan, stop that! / Claudia Mills.
        p. cm.
    Summary: Seventh-grader Alex Ryan enjoys attracting attention,
though he never seems to impress his father, but when his antics
cause problems with his would-be girlfriend on a school outing, he
has second thoughts about his actions.
    ISBN 0-374-34655-0
    [1. Schools—Fiction.   2. Interpersonal relations—Fiction.
3. Behavior—Fiction.   4. Fathers and sons—Fiction.]   I. Title.

PZ7.M63963 Aj 2003
[Fic]—dc21

                                                        2002025009

For Noreen and Alan Bernstein, with love

Alex Ryan, Stop That!

1

ALEX RYAN TOOK THE LAST SEAT in the back row of the West Creek Middle School multipurpose room. It was the perfect seat. He would be able to make all the funny comments he wanted to the other seventh graders, well out of hearing of any parents or teachers. And he would be as far as possible from his dad. Alex's dad always chose the center of the first row so that when he made his own comments he could stand up and turn around to address the entire audience. Alex hoped his dad wasn't going to make any comments tonight. But he knew his dad would. He always did.

The West Creek principal, Dr. Stanley, walked up to the microphone. "Good evening, parents, West Creek seventh graders," he said. The mike wasn't working right, so his last words were drowned in a deafening high-pitched squeal.

"I guess he didn't get his Ph.D. in audiovisual," Alex said.

Sitting in front of him, Marcia Faitak giggled. She was an extremely pretty girl, with wavy dark hair and large blue eyes. Tonight, however, Alex could see that she had a pimple on her forehead that was covered by pink stuff and the artful arrangement of her bangs.

The music teacher hurried over to adjust something on the sound system.

"Let's try this again," Dr. Stanley said. "Good evening, parents, West Creek seventh graders. Can everybody hear me?"

"Yes," some of the parents chorused.

"No!" Alex called out, though the mike was now working just fine. He couldn't resist seeing what would happen. As a few parents turned around to see who had spoken, Alex put on an expression of dumb bewilderment. The two boys sitting closest to Alex, Ethan Winfield and Julius Zimmerman, were obviously trying not to laugh out loud. Dave Barnett gave a satisfying guffaw.

The music teacher stepped up to adjust the mike again.

"Is that better?" Dr. Stanley asked.

"Too loud!" a parent shouted.

"How's this?" Dr. Stanley asked.

"Good!" The parents were sounding a bit impatient.

Alex restrained the urge to yell, "I still can't hear!" Sometimes he and Dave competed with each other to see how much class time they could waste with worthless comments, but Alex didn't think he could get away with any more right now.

"What?" Alex asked, just loudly enough for the back corner to hear. "Could you repeat the question?"

Dave burst out laughing and Marcia giggled again, but Alex thought Ethan and Julius were starting to look annoyed. They were best friends and reacted the same way to most things. Maybe the joke was becoming a bit stale. Alex decided to listen to what Dr. Stanley was trying to say.

"It is my pleasure to welcome you all to information night for the seventh-grade outdoor ed experience," Dr. Stanley went on. "In less than two weeks we'll be off to Elliot Ranch, from May twentieth to May twenty-third, for four days in the beauty of Colorado's high country. The seventh-grade teachers are all coming with us—I think they're starting to get some extra sleep, in preparation."

Some of the parents laughed.

"So are we," Alex said. "During math class."

Dave joined in with a long, loud snore. The snore was an extra good one, and a number of the seventh graders burst out laughing. Alex was glad to see that Ethan and Julius were laughing this time, too.

"Every part of the curriculum has been integrated into outdoor ed this year," Dr. Stanley said, sending a warning glance their way. "We'll be collecting soil and water samples: science. Graphing our results: mathematics. Looking at ancient Indian ruins: social studies. Keeping nature journals: English, art. Have I missed anything? Oh, the kids are studying first aid in their family-living classes, which I hope they *won't* need. And recipes for large-group cooking, which I know they *will* need. Our hikes will serve as P.E."

It actually did sound like fun. Alex had hated the sleep-away camp he had gone to last summer, but it would be kind of cool to go away for four days with all the West Creek kids. And four days of outdoor ed was definitely preferable to four days of indoor ed. Alex loved being outdoors. The best part of his life was running with the track-and-field team.

Alex tuned out as Dr. Stanley explained the details of the program. Casting about for something to do, he gave a quick tug at Marcia's hair, then swiftly resumed his expression of exaggerated innocence when she whirled around.

"I know that was you, Alex," she said. She was plainly trying to act mad, but Alex knew she wasn't really. The blue of her eyes exactly matched the blue of her tiny little tank top.

"*What* was me?"

"*You* know."

Alex shrugged, as if to say: "I haven't the faintest idea what you're talking about."

When Marcia faced forward again, Alex gave another tug, this time to the wild, red curls of the girl sitting next to Marcia, tiny, brainy Lizzie Archer. Lizzie yelped and clutched her curls protectively. She didn't turn around, but Marcia did. This time Marcia looked genuinely angry. Alex could tell that she didn't mind if he pulled *her* hair, but she didn't want him pulling another girl's hair.

"Ethan did it," Alex said.

"I did not!" Ethan protested.

"Boys," the principal called out. "Settle down back there." To the parents, he said, "I think these kids are ready for outdoor ed *now*. All right, parents, any questions?"

Lots of hands shot up, including Alex's dad's. Alex hated it when his dad spoke up at school meetings. Usually the questions started with some supposedly amusing remark about "my son, Alex," which Alex didn't find amusing at all. He knew his dad prided himself on coming to school events, even though he was a super-busy lawyer in downtown Denver. Sometimes Alex wished he'd stay at his office instead, especially on the track-meet days.

Luckily, Dr. Stanley called on another parent first, a mother who asked about the cost of the program and if there was any financial aid available. Alex didn't recognize her, but he could only imagine how embarrassed *her* kid must feel. Why didn't she just scream at the top of her lungs, "We're poor! We're poor!"

"How much adult supervision will there be?" another mom asked.

"We plan on having at least one parent for every twelve students," Dr. Stanley said. Alex hoped one of the parents wouldn't be his dad.

Then Alex heard Dr. Stanley call on his father. He steeled himself for what would come next.

Sure enough, his father turned to face the audience, as Alex had known he would. "I have three questions," he said. Alex could have predicted that, too. Once his father had the floor, he held on to the floor.

"First, West Creek's standardized test scores this year lagged behind East Creek's by three percentile points. Don't you think instructional time should be spent building test-taking skills rather than traipsing around in the woods, scribbling in 'nature journals'?"

The principal gave a long, droning answer to that one. Through it all, Alex's dad looked mildly amused, as if to say, "Gotcha!"

"Second, how much taxpayer money is paying for this?"

Dr. Stanley gave another long-winded answer that didn't seem to satisfy Alex's dad.

"Third, don't you think four days is too long for some of the kids? The last time my son, Alex"—here it came—"went to a sleep-away camp, he called home partway through, begging us to come and get him." He gave a low chuckle. Some of the other parents joined in appreciatively. "I mean, we're talking about kids here who still sleep with teddy bears, some of them."

Alex felt himself flushing a painful, dull red. He hadn't *begged* to come home from the camp last summer; he had *asked*. And that camp had been awful: all the other kids had seemed to know everybody, and he hadn't known anybody, and he had gotten off to a bad start with this one mean counselor on the first day.

And he *didn't* sleep with Mr. Bear, he just had him on his bed. Under his bed, usually. Mr. Bear didn't count as a teddy bear. He was more like a punching bag, when Alex needed to hit somebody. Or a pillow, when Alex needed something to squeeze. His mother called Mr. Bear a "comfort object." She had an old stuffed bunny as her comfort object. Alex's seventeen-year-old sister, Cara, had Kirsten, her favorite American Girl doll. Everybody in Alex's family had a comfort object, except for Alex's dad.

His dad didn't need comfort objects, but everyone who lived with him did. There was food for thought there.

"I think our students are ready for this," Dr. Stanley replied. "And certainly parents are more than welcome to join us. And teddy bears, too," he added with a smile.

Now they would all think Alex slept with a teddy bear. He waited for one of the guys to make a crack. Alex knew what *he* would have said if one of *their* parents had made the teddy bear remark. "What's your bear's name, Zimmerman?" "Have you been sewing lots of cute little clothes for your teddy, Winfield?" "How's Teddy-Weddy, Barnett?" None of the guys said anything. Alex had a terrible thought: they felt sorry for him.

Finally Dr. Stanley called on another parent. Alex didn't listen to the question.

Marcia turned around. "I sleep with a bear, too," she confided. "His name is Puffles."

Puffles? I sleep with a bear, *too*?

Dave couldn't hold back any longer. "What's *your* bear's name, Alex? Wuffles?"

Alex tried to think of something funny to say, something that would make clear to the others that he didn't sleep with a teddy bear, had never slept with a teddy bear, and never would sleep with a teddy bear. For once, his gift for comedy failed him.

As Marcia turned toward Lizzie, she touched her bangs on their strategic place over the pimple on her forehead. Even though Alex knew Marcia had only been trying to help, he had to lash out at somebody. He couldn't just *sit* there, in utter humiliation and shame.

"Hey, Faitak," Alex said, loud enough for the others to hear.

"What?"

"I think you have some kind of a puffle on your forehead. Is that a beesting? Or an insect bite? Or—wait—it couldn't be a *zit*, could it?"

Marcia stared at him. Then her face crumpled. She jumped up from her folding chair, pushed her way to the aisle, and ran out into the hall.

Great. Girls couldn't take a joke. But the stricken look on Marcia's face had given Alex a sick feeling in the pit of his stomach. He felt even worse, if that were possible, than he had before.

"What did you say to her?" Ethan asked. Ethan could get on this knight-in-shining-armor kick, where it was his mission to rescue all damsels in distress—usually from remarks made by Alex. There was a time when Ethan was always rescuing Lizzie. Now, apparently, he was going to start rescuing Marcia.

Alex thought fast. The best defense is a good offense, his dad liked to say. "All I said was, 'I think Ethan Winfield likes you.' "

"Right," Ethan said.

Alex knew that Ethan and Julius didn't really like him. It wasn't as if he liked them all that much, either. Despite the Wuffles remark, he and Dave were pretty good friends, and the girls liked him, too, especially Marcia. Or at least she *used* to. Why had he made that stupid crack about her pimple? He wouldn't have done it if his dad had known when to quit.

Alex didn't want to go away with these kids for four days to outdoor ed, with everybody asking him why he hadn't brought his dumb bear. He wanted to transfer to a different school, in a different state. And with a different family. Well, maybe he'd keep his mother and sister. But he wanted a different father. A different father, definitely.

2

"HOW WAS THE MEETING?" Alex's mom asked as Alex and his dad came from the garage into the kitchen. A freshly frosted cake stood on the counter, ready to be taken to West Creek the next day for a PTO fundraiser.

"It had its moments," Alex's father said. "There are a few of us parents holding their feet to the fire."

Alex's mother shot a quick look at Alex; he knew she wanted to ask him how the meeting had *really* been. But all she said was, "I made another cake for us, but it's not frosted yet. Give me ten more minutes, okay?"

Other mothers baked cakes for a school bake sale from mixes, if they baked at all. It was typical of Alex's mother to bake two cakes, one for the bake sale and one for home, both from scratch, each one decorated like a cake on the cover of a cooking magazine.

"Where's Cara?" Alex's dad asked. Cara was a junior at Summit High School.

Alex's mother hesitated for a split second before she answered. "Out with some friends."

"You mean, out with Dax."

"She said she'd be back by nine."

Alex's father looked at his watch. "Eighteen more minutes. What earring was Romeo wearing tonight? The diamond stud? Or the little pink flower?"

Alex's mom picked up her spatula. "I didn't notice. Out of the kitchen, you two. I can't frost cakes with an audience. Is your homework done, Alex?"

"Uh-huh. Almost."

"Go finish it."

Alex went upstairs to his room and opened his math book. He was a good math student—not a brain, like Lizzie Archer, but he could usually get A's in math without trying very hard. In ten minutes, he had the last two problems finished.

Did he have time to down a piece of cake before Cara got home? He didn't particularly want to be there when she arrived, especially if she was late. Alex's dad couldn't stand Cara's new boyfriend, Dax. Some of his dad's comments about Dax were funny, but Alex liked him. He thought Dax's lone earring, gleaming in his left ear, looked cool. Anyway, lots of guys had pierced ears.

"Cake!" his mother called upstairs. "Come and get it, if you want it."

He wanted it.

The clock on the microwave said 8:56 as Alex picked up his fork and took the first moist, delicious chocolate bite. He saw his mother steal a glance at the clock, too.

"I bet outdoor ed is going to be fun," she said.

"It'll be okay, I guess," Alex said, over a mouthful of cake. Maybe the other kids would have forgotten about his bear by then.

"Your dad is going to try to arrange his schedule so he can go, too."

Alex swallowed his bite in one angry gulp and shoved away the rest of his cake, uneaten. "Why? Why does he have to go?"

"He doesn't have to go, he wants to go."

"*Why?* It's, like, he has to go to *everything*? It's not enough that he ruins every track meet, now he has to ruin outdoor ed, too?"

"Honey, they need parent volunteers. You're lucky that your dad cares enough to do these things, even if . . . Well, I know he gets carried away sometimes. But it means so much to him to be involved in your activities; his own dad was always too busy."

Alex looked at her. Did she really think he was *lucky* that his dad was planning to go to outdoor ed? He couldn't believe she did. She had been trying to warn him, in her quiet, tactful way. But she hadn't been at the last track meet. She hadn't heard Dad berating the coach, shouting stuff at the other team, making cracks when Alex missed his last high jump.

"Why don't *you* come instead? *You* come."

"Oh, honey. The way your dad and Cara are getting along these days . . ."

Alex heard the car in the driveway. The clock on the microwave said 9:03. That wasn't late enough to trigger a scene between Cara and their dad, was it?

Cara appeared in the kitchen, without Dax. So far, so good. Alex caught a quick glimpse of Dax outside the door, his long hair pulled back in a ponytail, blowing her a goodbye kiss. He was wearing the diamond stud.

"I'm back!" Cara announced brightly. "I didn't turn into a pumpkin."

Standing side by side, she and their mother looked like sisters. Same short, slim build; same thick, shoulder-length, blond hair. Alex looked more like his dad: tall, broad in the shoulders, light brown hair cut super-short once a month by an old-fashioned barber with a candy-cane pole in front of his shop.

Cara asked, too casually, "Where's Dad?"

"On the computer. Taking care of some e-mail for work."

"I'd better head upstairs, too. I still have French to do for tomorrow." Cara reached over and patted Alex's head in the way that annoyed him most. "Cheer up. It can't be that bad."

"Finish your cake," his mother said to him, once Cara had gone. Alex heard the note of relief in her voice. Another family feud avoided.

Glumly Alex reached for his fork. He might as well eat the cake. If his father was really going to come to outdoor ed, he would need all the strength he could get.

At least the next day was Friday. One more day until the weekend. Then one more full week until outdoor ed. And after outdoor ed, just two more weeks until summer vacation.

Alex's mom drove him to school, picking up Dave on the way. She was one of the few seventh-grade moms who didn't work. Work "outside the home," that is. She didn't like it when people said she didn't work. She thought running a home, raising two kids, and volunteering at their schools *was* real work.

"I wish outdoor ed was next week," Dave said, slumping down in the backseat next to Alex.

"Me too," Alex said, though now he wasn't sure he did.

"Another whole week of regular school." Dave moaned. "We need to think of something to *do*. We need a *plan*."

"Your plan could be to study hard and do the best you can on all your final work," Alex's mother offered. Both boys ignored her. It was obvious that she was joking. At least, Alex hoped she was joking.

He still felt depressed about the outdoor ed meeting—his dad's crack about the teddy bear, his own crack to Marcia about the zit on her face. How was he supposed to let Marcia know he was sorry without actually coming out and saying he was sorry? Because here was one time when an apology would only make things worse. "That crack I made about the ugly red pimple on your forehead? The one you were hoping nobody would notice? Well, I'm sorry I made it."

Still, Alex tried to rouse himself for Dave's sake. If Dave wanted a plan, Alex would come up with a plan.

"Okay, here's the plan," he said.

"What?" Dave's face brightened with anticipation.

Alex's plans were always good ones. And this one, devised in less than half a minute, promised to be one of his best.

"I don't think I want to hear this," Alex's mother said. Luckily, they had reached the middle school. "Remember, they won't let you go to outdoor ed if your behavior isn't up to West Creek standards."

"Oh, Mom. Chill."

"Thanks for the ride, Mrs. Ryan." Dave was a big one for "please" and "thank you" around parents.

They got out of the car, and Alex's mom drove away.

"Well?" Dave asked.

"Our mission, if we are willing to accept it, is to see how many times we can get a teacher to use class time discussing underwear. We start today, finish a week from today. Underwear Week at West Creek Middle School. Are you ready to join me in accepting the mission?"

"I'm in." Dave burst out laughing. "Ryan, did anyone ever tell you you were crazy? Completely crazy?"

Alex grinned. "I believe you may have mentioned it from time to time."

He felt better already.

First period Alex had P.E., his favorite subject. He decided to postpone implementing the underwear plan until second period. Coach Krubek was the one teacher Alex didn't want to annoy.

That day they were doing a long-distance run around the school neighborhood. It was a perfect May morning, with new soft-green leaves on every tree and lilacs in bloom everywhere. Alex started out a little too fast, as he always did, then slowed down to pace himself. His feet hit the pavement in an easy, rhythmic stride. After the first mile or so, he got the same feeling he always did: that he could run like this forever, strong, steady, not talking to the guy next to him, not even thinking, just feeling his heart beat, feeling his chest rise and fall with his breathing, moving one foot after the other. Life was so simple when he was running.

Life stopped being simple in second-period English. They were in the middle of a unit on poetry.

"All right," Ms. Singpurwalla said. "I'll give you ten minutes to write something in your poetry notebooks. Then we'll spend the rest of the time talking about the form of a sonnet."

Alex opened his poetry notebook. Didn't you have to be *inspired* to write a poem? How could Ms. S. expect them to pull out a pen and just start writing? He'd rather look at Ms. S. than write. She was Alex's only good-looking teacher: young, with dark hair and dark eyes, usually dressed in a sexy-looking sari.

He snuck a look at Marcia, who was in his English class, too. He tried to catch her eye to offer a sheepish, hangdog grin, but she was staring in the opposite direction. As far as he could tell, her pimple looked a little better. Maybe she had squeezed it, though his mother always said not to.

"Alex," Ms. S. called to him in her low, musical voice. "This is our time to write."

"I don't know what to write about."

Then suddenly he did. Of course. On the top of his blank page he wrote the title to his poem, "Ode to Underwear." They hadn't studied odes yet in the poetry unit, but he had learned about them from Lizzie

Archer. She was always writing odes. She used to write them to Ethan. For a while last fall, Alex had thought that maybe Lizzie had been writing odes to *him*. The idea wasn't as terrible as he would have expected it to be. But then she switched her affections to Tom Harris, another brain.

Alex turned back to his own poem. Poets were always using flowery words to describe things. What was a flowery word for underwear? Alex tried to think of any ads he had seen. A lot of ad writers were poetic in their word choices, too. *Intimate apparel.* Ha! That was good. Alex wrote it down. And there was some other French-sounding word for underwear. It came to him. But how did you spell it?

This was Alex's moment. Hoping Dave was paying attention, he waved his hand. "How do you spell *longer-ray*?"

"*L-i-n-g-e-r-i-e,*" Ms. S. said, apparently without thinking.

Across the room, Dave gave his trademark guffaw. Dave had a great laugh. Someone should hire him for a laugh track on a sitcom.

Alert now, Ms. S. came over to Alex's desk and glanced down at his paper. He looked up at her, all wide-eyed innocence. After all, she herself had said that a poem could be on any subject, that no object was too ordinary or insignificant to be the topic of a poem.

"Let's find you another topic," Ms. S. said, her voice gentle but firm. So some topics *were* unsuitable for poetry.

"Like what? What's wrong with underwear? Why can't I write a poem about underwear?"

Ignoring the question, Ms. S. suggested, "You're a runner, aren't you? I've seen you out with the track team. Why don't you write a poem about running?"

Alex shook his head. The way he felt about running was private.

"How about springtime, then? 'Ode to Spring.' "

Oh, man.

Two minutes later, the poem was done. It had turned out pretty well, all things considered.

Ode to Spring

O spring!
The snow is slushy.
The mud is mushy.
How I sneeze
In the breeze.
I blow my nose
On my clothes.
My nose snorts
On my boxer shorts.
O spring!
O spring!

"Does anyone want to share his or her poem with the rest of the class?" Ms. S. asked.

Alex waved his hand. Ms. S. didn't call on him. She called on Lizzie, who had a poem about a daffodil whose fragile golden blossoms had been eaten by a hungry newborn deer.

He caught Marcia glancing his way and tried his sheepish, hangdog grin again. Marcia looked through him as if he weren't there.

ALEX AIMED AT SCORING one more underwear reference before lunch.

Third-period math with Mr. Grotient was pretty hopeless, unless Alex could come up with a word problem: "Let x equal the number of bras on sale this week at Target. Let y equal the number of Jockey briefs sold since November . . ."

Alex gave up there. He was good at math, but not *that* good. Maybe he could ask Lizzie to help him think of how to use algebra to combine x units of bras and y units of Jockey briefs in some clever way.

He looked at Lizzie, staring down at her paper with intense concentration, as if the math problem in front of her were another poem she was writing in the notebook she carried everywhere. Now wasn't the best time to ask Lizzie to help devise an underwear word problem.

Marcia was in math class, too, but Alex wasn't about to ask her for help, either. Definitely not for help in math. And definitely not for help today.

Fourth-period social studies was more promising. They were learning about the ancient peoples of North America, such as the Anasazi, the cliff-dwelling people who had lived in the dry canyons of the Southwest while Europe was still in the Dark Ages.

That day Mrs. Martin, their kindly, plump, middle-aged teacher, started talking about the everyday life of the Anasazi. Alex saw his opening. What was more a part of everyday life than underwear? Alex's mom made him change his own underwear every single day, even if it was perfectly clean.

Alex waited patiently until Mrs. Martin started talking about the clothing that would have been worn by the Anasazi: animal skins in winter; in summer, practically nothing.

Alex waved his hand. This time Dave started laughing before Alex had a chance to say anything. "What about underwear? Did they wear underwear?" Alex asked.

Dave wasn't the only one snickering now.

"Certainly both men and women wore loincloths most of the time in the summer," Mrs. Martin said, making a valiant effort to ignore the general level of hilarity in the room. "I'm not sure whether they continued to wear them in the winter, underneath their other garments. What's really interesting, I think, is that the Anasazi used the supple bark of the juniper tree to make soft, absorbent diapers for their babies."

"Did they wash them?" Dave called out. "Or just throw them out and make new ones? You know, like disposables?"

Alex had been wondering whether Dave was going to make any underwear contributions of his own, or be content to admire Alex's. He was glad to have Dave's help in keeping the conversation going.

"Oh, this was not a culture in which anything was discarded that could be used again. We're a long way from Pampers here, believe you me. Any other questions?"

Alex couldn't think of any. Apparently Dave couldn't, either. But they had already achieved their goal.

After fifth-period lunch came sixth-period family living. Earlier in the year, the class had done sewing, cooking, and some simple home repairs. Now they were doing first aid, to prepare for outdoor ed.

In family living, Marcia was going to have to acknowledge Alex's existence in some way. Alex, Marcia, Ethan, Julius, Lizzie, and a girl named Alison Emory all sat together at the same table as part of the same make-believe family; they had worked together, the six of them, since the first day of school.

Alex wasn't sure he was ready for family living today. Marcia wasn't in his social studies class, so fourth period had been a welcome break from guilt.

"Class," Ms. Van Winkle said in her brisk, energetic way. "Today we are going to practice bandaging a broken arm. We bandage a broken arm in order to immobilize the joint and prevent further injury. I'll put you in pairs to begin practicing."

Alex's heart sank. With his luck, he'd get Marcia as his partner. He just knew it.

Partly to stall for time, partly to carry out the plan, even though Dave wasn't in the same family-living class, Alex once again waved his hand in the air. He was becoming quite the participant in class activities.

"Yes, Alex?" Ms. Van Winkle for some reason seemed less than thrilled to be calling on him. But she couldn't possibly know that he had underwear on his mind.

"If we don't have a first-aid kit with us, what should we do to make bandages? Should we take off our clothes and rip them into pieces?"

Sitting next to Alex, Julius gave a low chuckle.

"Actually, that's a good question," said Ms. Van Winkle. "It would depend on the seriousness of the injury, of course, but if you needed to immobilize a joint and you had no other materials at hand, yes, I'm sure your parents would understand if you sacrificed an article of clothing. T-shirts or undershirts would probably work best for this purpose."

Satisfied, Alex made a mental note to tell Dave. *Undershirts*, he said to himself. Undershirts counted as underwear.

"All right, then. Let's get started." Ms. Van Winkle began to circulate from table to table, distributing rolls of bandages and assigning partners. Alex made sure that he practically had his arm around Julius when Ms. Van Winkle stopped at their table. Julius was a klutz, but better Julius than Marcia. Better *anyone*, today, than Marcia.

"Alison, work with Lizzie. Ethan, you work with Julius. Alex, work with Marcia."

It was little comfort that he had been right. Any way you looked at it, he was doomed. There must be a curse on the Ryan family. His sister was cursed to have a boyfriend whom their father detested. Alex was cursed to spend the next forty minutes bandaging and being bandaged by a girl who was perfectly justified in hating him. Would she even be willing to touch him? It would be hard to bandage a person without touching him.

Alex took the plunge. "Do you want to bandage me first, or should I bandage you?"

For answer, Marcia stuck her arm out toward him in icy silence, as she continued to stare fixedly in the opposite direction.

Alex decided to pretend he didn't notice that Marcia

was giving him the silent treatment. He'd be his usual amusing self, and perhaps she'd come around. Until his unfortunate zit remark, he and Marcia had always gotten along pretty well. It had been flattering to have the prettiest girl in the seventh grade asking him to dance at school dances. And once Dave had intercepted a note Marcia was passing to her best friend, Sarah Kessel. "Don't you think Alex Ryan is soooo cute?" the note had said. Marcia wasn't acting as if she thought Alex was cute now.

"Which arm is broken, madam?"

Marcia emphatically wiggled the arm she had already thrust out at him.

"It doesn't look broken, madam."

"Well, it is," Marcia snapped at him. At least snapping was speaking.

"Um . . . could you bend it a little? I have to get it in a sling, you know."

Marcia moved her outstretched arm and let it hang at an awkward angle. It did look broken now.

"Aha!" Alex said. "What is this I see? Can it be—a broken arm in need of bandaging?" He could tell Marcia was struggling not to smile.

Alex paused a bit longer to check out the rest of their family-living team. Smart, sensible Alison had already wrapped her bandage around Lizzie's arm as neat as neat could be. Julius was still bandaging Ethan's arm; that bandage hung off Ethan in crazy, tangled loops.

"Nice bandage, Zimmerman," Alex said. He couldn't help himself.

Julius grinned sheepishly. This was not the first time someone had pointed out to Julius that he was a klutz. And as often as not, that someone was Alex.

Alex started wrapping Marcia's arm, beginning with the hand. It felt odd to be touching a girl's smooth, bare skin in such a matter-of-fact way. Was she thinking the same thing? Was she glad, after all, that they had gotten each other as arm-bandaging partners? He made himself look at her face, trying not to let his eyes fall on her forehead.

"Ow!" Marcia said, jerking her supposedly broken arm away. With her other hand, she smoothed her bangs firmly in place. She was certainly showing no great signs of gladness.

"Ow?" Alex grabbed Marcia's arm back again. "A broken arm is always somewhat painful, madam."

"You're supposed to be putting on a *bandage*, not a *tourniquet*. You're cutting off all the blood to my fingers."

Alex didn't think his bandage was that tight. "Madam wants *blood* in her fingers?"

As if out of habit, Marcia gave one half-giggle. But she still looked close to tears.

Ms. Van Winkle bustled over to check their work.

"Excellent, Alison. Let's see your arm, Ethan."

Alex waited to see what she would say to Julius.

Julius, I'd advise you never to perform first aid on any-one unless you want a lawsuit on your hands. Alex knew all about lawsuits from his dad. He knew about humiliating cracks from his dad, too.

"Julius, I don't think Ethan's arm is really immobilized. Ethan, can you move your hand?"

Ethan waggled his fingers so vigorously that the entire bandage slipped off his arm and lay in loose coils on the floor.

"Yes," Alex answered for Ethan. "He can move his hand."

"Try it again, Julius," Ms. Van Winkle told him. She turned to project her voice to the whole class. "Remember, when you go to outdoor ed the week after next, you may very well need these skills. If you're out in the wilderness with no medical personnel nearby, *your* skills may mean the difference between someone's life and death."

Under his breath, Julius said to their team, "For some reason, I don't find that comment reassuring."

"Man," Alex said. "If the difference between someone's life and death depends on Zimmerman, then . . ." Instead of completing the sentence, he drew his fingers across his throat in a sinister knifelike motion.

Alison smiled politely, but Alex felt that his remark had generally fallen flat. Julius had already pretty much conceded that he stank at first aid.

"Alex, how are you doing with Marcia?"

Terrible, Alex thought, but didn't say anything.

"It's too tight," Marcia said miserably.

Ms. Van Winkle bent over for a closer look. "You want the bandage tight enough to keep the arm and hand from moving, but not so tight you cut off circulation." She turned to the class. "Make sure your bandages aren't *too* tight. If you cut off blood flow, you can do permanent damage to the hand. The first rule of first aid is not to make the injury even worse."

As Ms. Van Winkle hurried off to the next group, Alex tried to think of something funny to say so the others wouldn't think he had been bothered by the teacher's remarks. What could he say? Something else about underwear? If only Dave were in his family-living family instead of Ethan or Julius. Instead of Marcia. Was she ever going to give up sulking over one little comment about one little zit?

In seventh-period science class, there seemed no way to work underwear into the lab, which involved testing the pH of different common substances, like vinegar and milk. In eighth-period chorus, when they were singing "Some Enchanted Evening" from *South Pacific*, Alex changed the first line to "Some enchanted girdle." The guys standing nearest to him started laughing. But he didn't sing it loud enough for crabby old Mrs. Overton to hear. Besides, Dave wasn't in chorus, so there was really no point.

Finally school was over. Alex hurried to the locker

room to change into his running shorts and sleeveless T-shirt. Ten minutes later, he was out running laps around the quarter-mile track with the rest of the team. At first, as he ran, he counted how many underwear references he had made: four, all told, including "Some enchanted girdle." Then he started thinking about the apology he hadn't made. Didn't Marcia know how sorry he was? How much longer was she going to make him pay?

Then the rhythm of the run took over, and Alex kept on going, feet pounding, heart pumping, losing track of how many laps he had completed, of how many he had left to go, blissfully thinking of nothing at all.

WHEN ALEX WOKE UP ON SATURDAY MORNING, he found a note on the kitchen table. "Good morning, honey! Dad's at work, I'm running errands, Cara's at gymnastics. Be good. I love you, Mom." Under the signature was a heart, and three x's and three o's for kisses and hugs.

Alex crumpled the note and sent it flying toward the wastebasket, but down deep he liked his mother's notes. The paper landed neatly in the basket. Two points! Too bad basketball season was over for the year.

He poured himself some of his mom's homemade granola and ate it with his fingers, no milk. A long, empty morning stretched ahead of him. He would go for a run, but he had done something funny to his left ankle at the end of practice yesterday, and Coach

Krubek had said to take the weekend off from training. He could work on his Anasazi report for social studies, but that was lame.

Just as he was about to call Dave to see if he felt like biking to the mall, the doorbell rang. It was Dax.

"Cara's not here. She's at gymnastics."

"Oh, yeah, I forgot. When'll she be back?"

The note hadn't said. Alex squinted at the clock: ten-thirty. "Soon?" he guessed.

"Can I wait for her here? Your dad's not around, is he?"

"No. I mean, sure. You can wait for her here."

Dax followed Alex into the kitchen. He was wearing a sleeveless black T-shirt and baggy jeans with holes in both knees. A battered paperback book was shoved into his back pocket. Alex's mother might not notice what earring Dax was wearing, but Alex did: some kind of red stone. A ruby? Alex doubted it was a real one.

Should he offer Dax something to eat? If so, what? "You hungry?"

"Nah. I just ate. So how's it going?"

"Okay."

Dax was a senior at the same high school as Cara, but he wasn't taking college prep classes; he was in vo-tech. That was even worse than the earring, in Alex's father's eyes.

"School's almost over," Dax said.

"Yeah. First we have to go to outdoor ed, though."

"Cool. Soon as I graduate, I'm planning to be outdoors every day for the rest of my life. No desk job for me."

"It'd be cooler if they weren't making us do all this other stuff while we're there. You know, nature journals, stuff like that." *And if my dad weren't going, too.*

"Sounds okay. Did you ever read *Walden*, by Thoreau? You could call it a nature journal, sort of. One of my favorite books."

Dax pulled the book from his pocket and opened it, seemingly at random: " 'The mass of men lead lives of quiet desperation,' " he read to Alex. "Is that true, or what?" He flipped through a few more pages. " 'Beware of all enterprises that require new clothes.' " He glanced down at his own torn pants, and grinned.

Alex hadn't known Dax was that much of a reader. He guessed he hadn't expected a vo-tech guy to love to read.

"My dad says he's coming. To outdoor ed. As one of the parent volunteers." Alex didn't know why he'd blurted that out. Maybe so Dax wouldn't go on and on about how much fun outdoor ed was going to be.

"Maybe he'll spend most of his time hanging with the other parents."

"Maybe."

"He sure hates my guts. I wouldn't care, but it's hard on Cara. I didn't know there were parent types who still got bent out of shape about a guy wearing an earring."

"It's not just the earring," Alex said. Then he wished he hadn't. He didn't want Dax to feel worse than he did already.

"I know, I know. I'm not going to *college*. I'm not going to— Where'd your dad go? He only told me six times."

"Cornell."

"That's right. I'm not going to *Cornell*. I'm going to work with my hands, out in the sun and the rain and the wind. I'll get myself a cabin in the woods somewhere, like Thoreau did, and just *live*. And if guys like your dad don't like it, that's too bad." Dax opened his book again: " 'Public opinion is a weak tyrant compared with our own private opinion. What a man thinks of himself, that it is which determines, or rather, indicates, his fate.' "

Alex wasn't sure what that was supposed to mean.

"It doesn't matter what other people think of you," Dax translated. "What matters is what you think of yourself."

Well, that was a convenient quote for someone like Dax, who obviously wasn't going anywhere in his life. It sure wasn't what Alex's dad believed.

Alex heard Cara's car in the driveway. Dax's face lit up. Alex couldn't imagine someone's face ever lighting up like that for him, not at the rate he was going.

Maybe he should ask Dax what to do about what he said to Marcia. It wasn't as if he had anyone else he could ask for advice about girls. But Dax probably would never have made a comment that stupid in the first place.

"Take care," Dax said. "Give Thoreau a try sometime."

"Okay," Alex said. He doubted that he would.

Dave wasn't home when Alex called. Alex tried a few other guys. They weren't home, either. Then Alex pulled out the school directory and looked up Marcia's number. Maybe he'd call her just to say hello, and after he'd said hello, she'd say hello, and they'd chat for a while about nothing in particular, and everything would be the way it had been before.

Alex dialed her number. But as soon as he heard Marcia's voice chirping "Hello?" he hung up. He couldn't go through with the call. He just couldn't.

The instant he put the phone down, it occurred to him that she might have Caller-ID. He could imagine the digital display lighting up, all in caps: ALEX RYAN. Alex was named after his dad, but he wasn't a junior. They had different middle names. His dad was Alexander Arthur. He was Alexander Anthony.

Oh, well. Maybe it would be okay if Marcia knew he had tried to call. Maybe calling a girl and hanging up when she answered the phone counted as saying you were sorry for hurting her feelings.

Alex clicked on the TV and then clicked it off again. He might as well take some notes for his report on the Anasazi. Alex liked to goof off as much as he could in class, but then get a good grade, anyway. His dad gave him too much grief if his grades weren't A's.

By lunchtime he had the whole first draft done. Not bad for two hours' work. He drifted downstairs to check in with his mom, back from her errands.

"Someone's been awfully quiet this morning," she said. "You haven't been sleeping all this time, have you?"

"Homework." Alex was conscious of the halo glowing around his head.

"Not playing games on the computer?"

"Homework," Alex repeated. "I got my social studies report practically done."

His mother looked impressed. Alex usually left any weekend homework until late on Sunday night.

"If I had some money, I could bike to the mall . . ."

"Hand me my purse."

Alex was happy to fetch it for her. From her wallet she pulled out a ten-dollar bill and handed it to him. He was off.

West Creek had great bike paths everywhere, so he could ride to the mall without worrying about cars.

Once there, he looked around to see if he could find any of the guys from school, and to make sure Marcia didn't somehow sneak up on him. Just as he was about to give up and eat alone, Julius and Ethan appeared at the entrance to the food court.

"Zimmerman! Winfield!" Alex was surprised by how glad he was to see them. They weren't even his friends, really, but they were vastly better than nobody. "You guys eating here?"

"We don't have any money," Julius said.

"I do. Ten bucks. That's enough for all of us. What do you want? Really, it's my mom's money," Alex added when he saw Ethan hesitate. "She'd want me to treat you guys."

They all ordered burgers. Alex felt so good to be sitting with kids who weren't mad at him, who weren't likely to *get* mad at him, that on impulse he said, "Tonight. You want to have a sleepover at my house?" His parents never minded when he had friends over: his mom, because she was so hospitable; his dad, because he wanted to be able to brag to other people about how popular his son was. Plus, his dad always liked having a captive audience.

Ethan shot a quick look at Julius. Now Alex was sorry he had asked. Couldn't either of these guys decide anything without consulting the other one? Just because they were best friends didn't make them Siamese twins.

"Sure," Ethan said, after a pause that went on a second too long. "I mean, I have to ask my parents first."

"I have to ask mine, too," Julius echoed.

Oh, forget it, Alex felt like saying. He didn't want to beg anybody to come to his house. If Ethan and Julius weren't all that thrilled about the sleepover, he wasn't, either.

But the invitation had already been issued. It was too late to back out now. As soon as he got home, he'd call Dave to see if he could come, too. With Ethan and Julius, Alex always felt like the odd man out. With Dave there, it would be two against two.

As soon as he got home from the mall, Alex called Dave again. But Dave couldn't come over that night: his grandmother was in town for a visit. So Alex was going to have to manage the sleepover without him. Both Ethan and Julius had left messages saying that they could come.

Ethan and Julius appeared at the door at eight o'clock, each with a small duffel and a sleeping bag. It didn't help that Alex's father was the one to greet them.

"Hey, boys, come on in. We don't bite, you know." He laughed heartily, as if he had just said something funny. "Come on, Alex, greet your guests. Take them upstairs and show them where to stow their gear."

Things started to look up when Alex's father retired

to his office and Alex's mother appeared with a tray of homemade brownies, fresh from the oven. And, luckily, Mr. Bear was well hidden under Alex's bed when they finally went to his room. Alex had taken pains to hide him. He had made sure his bed was unmade, too, and that some of his dirty clothes were strategically strewn across the floor. If Ethan and Julius thought he was a wuss after his dad's remark at outdoor ed, one look at his room would convince them that he was definitely a regular guy.

But the sleepover dragged. They played a bunch of Nintendo, but couldn't agree on a video. Ethan probably wasn't allowed to watch anything except *Mary Poppins*. And if Julius ever tried to operate a VCR, he would most likely tear up the tape. All the sewing machines in their family-living class at school broke permanently on the day Julius used them.

Alex had to think of something. Although his parents and Cara had already gone to bed, it was only eleven o'clock. Alex had never heard of a sleepover where people went to sleep before midnight.

"Hey, I have an idea!" he said. It was a good one, too—one that would cancel out his father's Mr. Bear remark forever. "My parents are asleep. Let's sneak out and T.P. somebody's tree."

He could already hear their answers: *Ooh, we're not supposed to do that. Ooh, my mommy will spank me if she finds out.*

Ethan looked at Julius, and Julius looked at Ethan. As usual.

"Like wrap it in toilet paper?" Julius asked.

"Duh."

"Whose tree?" Ethan asked.

This was encouraging. They hadn't said right out they wouldn't do it. They were probably as bored as Alex was. Besides, any kid would like to wrap a tree in toilet paper. Alex had been longing to do it ever since some guy who liked Cara had done it to their tree two years ago.

"Anyone's." Suddenly Alex had a truly brilliant idea. Marcia. If he wrapped her tree magnificently in toilet paper, she'd *have* to forgive him for everything. "Maybe Faitak," Alex said carefully, trying not to sound too eager.

"Won't her parents mind?" Julius asked.

"We'll ask their permission first." Alex threw up his hands. "Guys! Parents mind everything."

"I guess we could kind of be walking by their house tomorrow morning and help clean it up," Ethan suggested.

Right. *Hi, Marcia. Hi, Mr. and Mrs. Faitak. We just happened to be walking by to see if you had any toilet paper wrapped all over your tree that we could help you clean up.* These two were hopeless.

"It's not that big a deal to clean it up," Alex said, trying to keep the impatience out of his voice. "It'll all blow off the first time it's really windy. It'll look great! Like a work of art. Like a tree with bee-you-ti-ful white lace all over it."

"Bee-you-ti-ful white lace made out of toilet paper," Julius said.

To Alex's relief, Ethan cracked up. The plan was a go.

Alex found six rolls of toilet paper under the sink in the bathroom down the hall that he and Cara shared. He stuffed them in his backpack with his set of house keys. Then, with exaggerated stealth, the three boys tiptoed downstairs in their stocking feet. The carpet on the stairs was so thick no footsteps could be heard.

Slowly, carefully, Alex eased open the front door. It was almost midnight, and their deserted cul-de-sac was deathly quiet. A slight breeze stirred: the chilly air on Alex's face felt moist and fresh, after the stuffiness of the house. This was so great!

Alex led the way, once they had all hastily shoved their feet into their shoes, the other boys following. A car went by, driving fast. That was how Alex would drive someday, when he had a car of his own. His dad had bought Cara her own car the day she turned sixteen.

They reached Marcia's home—a sprawling brick house with half the rooms built over a huge three-car garage. There was a large tree on the front lawn, its leaves newly opened. Maybe an oak? Alex didn't know one tree from another. But he knew when a tree was perfect for wrapping.

"What do we do now?" Ethan asked.

Hadn't Ethan's older brother taught him *anything*? "You just throw the toilet paper roll over a branch, catch it, and then throw it again. Try not to make too much noise. We don't want anyone calling the police." Alex added the last line with deliberate nonchalance, as if he had extensive experience in dodging the long arm of the law. As soon as he said it, he realized it was a mistake.

"Let's go back," Julius said. He and Ethan turned to go.

"Guys." Alex knew he had to act quickly. He ripped at the toilet paper to free the edge of the roll and unrolled it several times. Then, holding on to the last sheet of paper with his left hand, with his right he hurled the roll in the general direction of the tree, then ran and caught it. The toilet paper unfurled in a long, satisfying arc. It was glorious to see. Alex threw it again, farther this time. The toilet paper gleamed ghostly in the moonlight.

"Here." He tossed a roll to Ethan and one to Julius.

In a moment, all three boys were throwing their rolls of toilet paper, higher and higher. Julius emitted one high-pitched giggle before Ethan pounced on him. But no lights came on in Marcia's windows.

Alex stepped back to admire the overall effect of

their handiwork. Pretty spectacular, though a number of upper branches were still uncovered. "I'm going up," he announced to the others. "Give me a boost."

Ethan laced his fingers into a stirrup, and Alex grabbed on to the lowest branch and swung himself up. Then he climbed cautiously upward, wrapping as he went. He could have peered into the upstairs bedroom windows, if the curtains had been open. He wondered which one was Marcia's. She was in for a surprise when she looked outside the next morning.

Would she guess he had done it? Alex Ryan, star of the West Creek track-and-field team. Alex Ryan, underwear king. Alex Ryan, host of the wildest sleepover ever.

Alex climbed out onto a narrow branch, bound and determined to wrap every last limb of Marcia's tree.

"Be careful!" Ethan cautioned from below in a loud whisper.

"Fear not, Bubba!" Alex mouthed back cockily.

Too cockily. On *Bubba*, the branch began to crack. Alex tried to swing himself to a sturdier branch, but it was too late. Under his struggling weight, the bough broke. Alex fell with it, through a blur of fluttering toilet paper, to the hard ground below.

FOR AN INSTANT ALEX LAY STILL, stunned by the impact of the whole left side of his body slamming into the ground. He was afraid he might throw up.

As Ethan and Julius came thundering over to him, a light flashed on in one of the upstairs windows.

Alex saw it first. In a hoarse whisper, he urged, "Run!"

"Are you okay?" Julius asked.

"Run!"

They ran.

Somehow Alex managed to stumble to his unsteady feet. His left shoulder and arm hurt incredibly. Maybe he had broken something. Better his arm than his leg. He couldn't run track with a broken leg. But he didn't have time to think about any of that now.

A huge pair of spotlights on the garage suddenly lit

up Marcia's front lawn. Shielding his face with his good arm, Alex took off after the others. A streamer of torn toilet paper, stuck fast to his shoe, trailed behind him as he fled.

He caught up with Ethan and Julius where they were waiting for him, two long blocks away.

"Man," Ethan panted.

"I don't think they saw me," Alex said. "At least, they didn't see my face."

"When that branch broke, I thought for sure it was curtains for you." Julius gave Alex a friendly whack on the shoulder. Unfortunately, it was his injured left shoulder.

Alex winced. "Take it easy. My left arm doesn't feel so good."

"You think it's broken?" Ethan asked.

"We could immobilize it," Julius suggested. " 'If you have no other bandaging materials handy, you can use—toilet paper!' "

All three boys started to laugh. It was probably relief at having escaped Marcia's parents, rather than the joke itself, but Alex's laughter came uncontrollably, in great gut-wrenching guffaws.

"I have one roll left," Ethan gasped out. He waved it triumphantly.

"Our toilet paper skills may mean—the difference between—life and death!" Julius bent double, clutching his stomach.

"Stop!" Alex moaned. "Laughing makes it hurt worse."

But none of them could stop. Ethan and Julius staggered to the closest lawn and rolled in the grass. Alex couldn't roll because of his shoulder, but he flung himself to his knees and beat the ground with his unhurt hand.

Finally they were laughed out. They lay on the damp grass, grinning at one another in the darkness.

"No one came after us," Alex said. "I think we're okay. If you can call a dislocated shoulder and a broken arm okay."

The three of them started laughing again.

"Do you really think it's broken?" Julius asked.

Alex tried wiggling the fingers of his left hand. They wiggled just fine. "Nah. If it was broken, I wouldn't be able to move my hand."

"So the only thing broken is their tree," Ethan said.

"And we've already bandaged it," Alex quipped.

Once again the boys launched into spasms of giddy laughter. But this time, when the laughter died down, the silence afterward felt different, strained.

"I wish we hadn't broken it," Ethan said. His words hung in the darkness.

Alex knew Ethan meant he wished that he, Alex, hadn't broken it. Alex wished he hadn't broken it, too. But he hoped the others weren't going to make a big thing about it.

"Look, this is Colorado. Tree branches break all the time. They break in the snow. They break in the wind. They just *break*."

"My dad had a tree guy come after one of our branches broke last May—you know, in that really heavy, wet snow," Julius said. "It cost three hundred dollars."

Alex definitely didn't like the way this conversation was going. Were Ethan and Julius going to suggest that he *pay* for the broken branch? Pay three hundred *dollars*? He didn't have three hundred dollars. And if he did, he wasn't about to spend it on a tree.

"So what did the tree guy do? Glue the broken branch back on?" Alex jeered.

"Evened it off," Julius said. "So it looked better."

"They didn't see us," Alex said, his voice cracking with mounting irritation. "Or maybe they saw us, but they couldn't see it was *us*. If you guys say anything about this to anybody . . ."

"We didn't say we were going to say anything." Ethan's voice was flat, depressed.

"Well, don't. And don't let it show in your face, either. You know how girls are. They keep at you about something until your face gives you away."

"Come on," Julius said, in an evident attempt to change the subject. "I'm tired. Let's go back."

Alex glanced at his watch. It was one-thirty. At least the sleepover had gone past midnight. He hoped it had been worth it. If those guys squealed, Alex would have something a lot worse than a bruised shoulder to worry about.

They walked the last two blocks in silence. Alex tried to put the damaged tree out of his thoughts. Probably nobody would even miss the stupid broken branch.

An enormous yawn overtook him. It would be good to go to bed. Maybe when he woke up in the morning, his shoulder wouldn't hurt as much.

"Hey," Julius said in a low, startled voice.

Alex looked up. Every window in the downstairs of his house was illuminated. And the silhouetted figure of his father was looming in the front door.

"Where have *you* been?" his father's voice boomed out. Apparently his father didn't care if he woke the whole neighborhood.

Alex knew that Ethan and Julius expected him to answer. He thought fast. It was hard to think of anything better than the truth. Why else would three guys be roaming around at one-thirty in the morning? They obviously weren't out returning overdue library books. At least Ethan had had the sense to stuff the telltale roll of leftover toilet paper under his shirt.

"We were T.P.ing someone's tree." Alex made himself look his father full in the face as he said it. His father hated it if he cringed; he despised cowardice.

"T.P.ing someone's tree. Oh, that is just brilliant."

The tone was sneering, but Alex could tell that his father wasn't really angry; he was just putting on a show for Ethan and Julius. Alex had a feeling that his dad had done his share of hell-raising in his day. He wasn't an angel, either.

"May I ask whose tree?"

"A girl at school."

"A sweetheart!" His dad's voice dripped with sarcasm.

Alex felt himself flushing. The T.P.ing hadn't been meant as a love letter but as an apology. Not that Alex could explain that to his dad.

"And who is the lucky lady?" his dad went on.

Should he tell? Should he lie? If he told, his dad might see the broken branch when he drove by, and then what? Of course, he didn't even have to tell: his dad could hardly miss the tree when he passed Marcia's house on the way to his Sunday morning golf game.

"Just a girl," Alex said.

"A mystery!"

His father was plainly enjoying himself. But Alex felt ready for bed. He stole a glance at Ethan and Julius. They looked dead on their feet, too, and they hadn't even survived a twenty-foot fall.

"I hope her parents are good sports," Alex's father said, sounding finally ready to wind down and let them in the house. Then something—the guilty look plastered all over Ethan's and Julius's faces?—made him turn toward Alex sharply. "Did they see you? Are they going to march over here tomorrow morning and read me the riot act?"

Alex felt his own face radiating guilt now. He was too tired to hide it. It was torture to be kept awake when you ached all over to sink into deep, blissful sleep.

"There's something you're not telling me. What is it?"

Alex gave up. "Well, one branch of the tree kind of broke."

" 'Kind of' broke? Did it break, or didn't it?"

"It broke."

"Great. You can't even throw toilet paper at some girl's tree without provoking a lawsuit. And how could you *break* a tree branch by throwing *toilet paper* at it?"

"I climbed up to do it, and the branch broke, and I fell."

"Brilliant," his dad said again. "My son, the genius."

Alex noticed that his dad wasn't asking whether he had been hurt in the fall. Too bad Ethan and Julius hadn't come back to wake his dad up at two in the morning and say, "Oh, Mr. Ryan, we have some terrible news. Your only son is dead." But probably his father would just have said, "Brilliant. My son can't even T.P. a tree without killing himself."

"It was our fault, too," Julius said.

"We'll go tell Marcia's parents in the morning,"

Ethan offered. "We can all chip in to pay the three hundred dollars for the tree guy."

Alex cringed. Leave it to Ethan to blab out Marcia's name the first time he opened his mouth. And even though Alex half welcomed their support, he half resented it, too. It hadn't been their fault at all. The T.P.ing had been his idea entirely.

"Wait a minute." Alex's father raised his voice again. "Don't you go squawking your heads off. Let me handle this. We could be looking at major litigation here. People go where the money is. Believe me. They sniff out and find the deep pockets. Three hundred dollars is nothing compared to what they'll be asking. You boys have done enough damage already. Let me take care of it from here."

"Yes, sir," Ethan and Julius said together. Alex's dad was the kind other kids called "sir."

"Okay. Go up to bed now."

Alex's mother was waiting for them in the hall, her eyes still sleepy, though her forehead was creased with worry. "Do you boys want anything before you go upstairs?" she asked gently. "Hot chocolate? I don't mind fixing you some."

"No, thanks," Alex said, sure he was speaking for the others, as well. Hot chocolate wasn't going to get them out of the mess they were in.

Feeling oddly close to tears, Alex led the way upstairs. Without another word, the boys lay down in their clothes, teeth unbrushed, Alex on his bed, Julius and Ethan in their sleeping bags on the floor.

Exhausted as he was, Alex couldn't fall asleep right away. He could tell from their tense, shallow breathing that Ethan and Julius were still awake, too. He had a feeling that Ethan's and Julius's dads would have handled things differently, made them go to Marcia's parents and apologize, made them pay what they owed. He thought his dad's way might be better. Certainly, apologies of any kind hadn't worked out well for him lately.

But there had been something in the look on Ethan's face as he mumbled his promise of silence that made Alex almost wish his father had reacted differently. He knew his dad's idea of "handling" things was to say nothing and hope Marcia's parents never found out. His dad always thought first and foremost like a lawyer. Just once, Alex wished he would think like—a dad.

MARCIA'S PARENTS DIDN'T SHOW UP at Alex's house Sunday morning. The boys slept till about ten, when Alex's mom made them blueberry pancakes and sausages for breakfast. She didn't say anything about the tree incident. She must have figured that a middle-of-the-night encounter with Alex's dad was punishment enough. Alex's shoulder was still sore, but it was obvious that it was going to be okay. Maybe the whole thing was going to be okay.

"See you tomorrow," Ethan said as he and Julius got on their bikes to pedal home.

"Adiós, amigo," Julius added.

Should Alex remind them not to tell anyone about the tree? He decided against it. He just gave a wave and let them ride off into the midday sun. He had a feeling they were going to talk about it the moment they were out of his hearing.

Riding to school on Monday morning with his mother and Dave, Alex was quieter than usual in the car, letting Dave do most of the talking.

"Underwear Week continues!" Dave proclaimed.

"Underwear Week? I didn't see this listed anywhere on the school calendar." Alex's mother sounded amused rather than annoyed.

Alex couldn't muster up Dave's enthusiasm. "I don't know. Maybe Underwear *Day* was enough?" He tried to put a positive spin on it. "One glorious day, to live forever in infamy!"

"So what's the next plan? We can't stop now, man. We're hot!"

But Alex couldn't think of anything right then. He felt drained, blocked. As if he had that writer's block that people talked about. Comedian's block, that was what he had. "I'll think about it," he said lamely.

Sure enough, after first period, on the way to English, Marcia stopped him in the hallway. "It was you," she said, standing directly in front of him to block his path. Her blue eyes were sparkling once again with teasing laughter. He could tell that, as he had predicted, she was pleased both that he had papered her tree and that she had found him out.

Except, thanks to her broken tree limb and his father's warning, he couldn't let her know that she had found him out.

He had to act dumb. "Huh?"

"Don't play innocent with me." She poked him playfully in the chest. "Did you or did you not toilet-paper my tree on Saturday night?"

If only he could play along, let her believe the answer that she wanted to believe, the answer that also happened to be true. But he couldn't. His father would kill him if he did. His dad was the reason he had gotten in trouble with Marcia in the first place; now his dad was the reason he couldn't get out of it.

"Get real," he said, forcing his voice to sound hard and cold. "Like I would waste perfectly good toilet paper on your tree? *Used* toilet paper, maybe. But nice new toilet paper fresh off the roll? Dream on."

As if it were a replay of their doomed conversation at the outdoor ed meeting, the friendly, flirting smile died from Marcia's face. "I hate you, Alex Ryan." She sounded as if she meant it.

Alex shrugged. The bell rang. Marcia spun on her heel and headed off to English. Since they were in the same class, Alex had no choice but to tag along behind her.

Ms. Singpurwalla called the class to attention. "Today we're going to take a little break from poetry."

"Yay!" someone at the back of the room hollered. Ms.

Singpurwalla's pretty face betrayed a hint of disappointment. She worked so hard to get her students to love poetry the way she did. But Alex, remembering how she had censored his finest attempt at an ode to underwear, refused to give in to pity.

"You'll be keeping nature journals at outdoor ed next week. So I want us to read some outstanding examples of famous nature journals and talk about what makes them so successful." She began passing out thick packets of photocopied journal entries.

Still feeling miserable, Alex looked down at the first entry. It was from *Walden* by Henry David Thoreau. That was mildly interesting, since Dax had mentioned it to him just two days ago. But when he started to read, he found himself tuning out. Was nothing in his life going to go right ever again? Thoreau got to live in a cabin in the woods, surrounded by nature. Alex had to go to school with a girl who now hated him. The only nature in his life was the tree limb he had broken and various piles of dog doo he had stepped in.

He found the last thought oddly cheering. He'd make his own journal, on animal droppings. *Animal Droppings I Have Stepped In.* He chuckled to himself. Maybe he didn't have comedian's block, after all.

By Thursday, Alex hadn't heard anything more about Marcia's tree, and his shoulder felt completely fine. Marcia still wasn't speaking to him. Even more humiliating than a crack about your camouflaged zit, apparently, was finding out that the boy you thought had a crush on you hadn't been the one who had toilet-papered your tree.

In family living that day, Alex perked up when he saw the movie screen pulled down behind Ms. Van Winkle's desk. Maybe they would see a gory film about first aid being administered to the victims of some horrific accident. Alex remembered, years ago, making Mr. Bear play the victim role in various natural and man-made disasters staged in his backyard. Mr. Bear was probably relieved to have been promoted from accident victim to comfort object. But then he'd been demoted to source of undying public humiliation.

"Don't get excited, she's just going to be using the overhead projector," Julius told Alex as Alex sat down at their table.

Marcia was chatting with Lizzie and Alison as if the boys weren't there. Alex remembered when smart, brainy, poetic Lizzie had been the class outcast. Now she was one of the popular girls. Marcia deserved some of the credit for that. If anyone knew how to turn someone into a popular girl, it was Marcia.

That day Marcia had her hair fixed in some new way, with a little clip thing holding it back from her face. Alex thought it looked pretty cute. Now she was trying out one of her clips on Lizzie's wild red curls. After Marcia was done with her, Lizzie looked cute, too.

"All right, class," Ms. Van Winkle said once the bell had sounded and Marcia had whisked her hair clips away. "Today we're going to be learning first aid for bites and stings."

A couple of weeks ago, Alex would have buzzed like a bee and given Marcia's arm a hard little "beesting" pinch, but today he refrained. He couldn't resist buzzing, but he kept his hands to himself. A low, droning hum joined in from some of the other tables. The classroom sounded like a meadow of clover in bloom, with a nectar-gathering bee perched on every blossom.

"It isn't so funny," Ms. Van Winkle said sharply, "when someone has an allergic reaction to a beesting and goes into anaphylactic shock. Do any of you know if you are allergic to beestings or insect bites?"

One boy raised his hand. Alex was impressed as Ms. Van Winkle gave the symptoms of allergic reaction to beestings: severe swelling of the eyes, lips, and tongue; severe itching; bluish tinge to the skin; dizziness; collapse. Listening to the list, Alex began to feel as if he had each symptom in turn. He thought about collapsing onto the floor, but decided against it.

"In cases of anaphylactic shock, you'll need to summon immediate medical attention," Ms. Van Winkle said. "For ordinary beestings, ice can help reduce swelling. But first check to see if the stinger is still in the skin. If it is, you'll need to try to remove it right away; scraping it off with a credit card or library card works well. Don't use tweezers. Tweezers just squeeze more venom into the wound."

Alex noticed that Lizzie was unusually pale. Maybe she would actually collapse onto the floor. That would make class considerably more interesting, but Alex liked Lizzie; he didn't want her to hurt her head, or anything. To distract her attention from Ms. Van Winkle's gruesome comments, he pretended to be yanking an enormous stinger out of his own arm.

"Ow! Ooh! Ouch!" he moaned, as if engaged in a fierce tug-of-war with the imaginary stinger. "There! I got it!" He recoiled backward and almost knocked over his chair.

"Alex," Ms. Van Winkle said, in her low, warning voice.

He checked Lizzie: she wasn't laughing, but the normal color had returned to her face.

"Next, we need to talk about poisonous spider bites," Ms. Van Winkle went on. "There are three main kinds of spider found in the United States that are poisonous to humans." She clicked on the overhead projector, and a huge, shiny spider appeared on the screen. "This is a black widow spider," she said.

Marcia gave a dainty squeal.

"Hi, Charlotte," Alex said. "How's Wilbur?"

"Charlotte wasn't a poisonous spider," Lizzie corrected.

Ms. Van Winkle showed pictures of the brown recluse spider and of the tarantula. None of them looked like something you'd want to encounter in a woodpile, or under the seat in an outhouse.

"I heard we'll be using outhouses at outdoor ed," Alex said. He couldn't help himself, even if it upset Lizzie. He had to do something to pass the time when he was sitting next to somebody who once had liked him, but now hated his guts. "I sure hope there aren't going to be any black widows crawling around in there. It would be pretty awful to get seated, all nice and comfortable, and then—"

"Stop it!" Marcia hissed, looking protectively at Lizzie. "Don't listen to him, Lizzie."

"Well, it *would* be awful," he said, "wouldn't it?"

Alex couldn't see much point in learning about spider bites, because the only treatment Ms. Van Winkle offered was, call for medical help and hope the victim doesn't die before it gets there. Well, Ms. Van Winkle said the part about calling for medical help; Alex added the last part himself.

"Take the spider with you, if possible," Ms. Van Winkle read from her notes.

Alex wasn't the only kid who burst out laughing at that one. "Hey, spidey-widey! Here, girl!" Alex called.

This time Ms. Van Winkle chose to ignore him. "With snakebite, too," she said, "it's important first of all to determine whether or not the snake in question is poisonous. There are four major kinds of poisonous snake in North America."

She switched the transparency on the overhead projector from a spider to a snake. "The kind we're most likely to encounter at outdoor ed is the rattlesnake. Note the slit-like eyes; the poison sac lies right behind them."

Alex gazed at the snake upon the screen with friendly interest. He had liked snakes ever since his mother had signed him up for a week-long science class on reptiles, the summer after second grade. One of his prized possessions was a real rattlesnake rattle from a snake his grandfather had killed on his ranch. Maybe Alex's snake rattle counted as a comfort object, too.

"I heard that some of the outhouses at outdoor ed have nests of rattlesnakes in them," Alex announced, to continue his humorous monologue on the subject of outhouses.

He glanced at the girls. Lizzie looked a bit white again. Marcia had apparently heard enough gruesome stories for one class. She had her notebook open and was making an elaborate doodle all over one page. It was a picture of a big-eyed princess type, with long flowing hair and huge tragic eyes, but better than most. It made sense that Marcia, who was so good at fixing people's hair, would also be good at drawing.

"Every year, forty thousand people are bitten by snakes in the United States," Ms. Van Winkle said. "But of these, only fifteen hundred incidents involve poisonous snakes."

"And only twelve hundred happen at outdoor ed," Alex added. He grinned at Lizzie to show that he was just kidding, and to his relief, she gave him a shaky smile back. Still engrossed in her drawing, or pretending to be, Marcia wasn't listening.

"Now, who knows the treatment for snakebite?" Ms. Van Winkle asked the class. "Does anyone know what to do?"

Tom Harris, the boy Lizzie seemed to like, raised his hand. "Don't you make an incision in the skin and, well, suck the venom out?"

This suggestion was greeted with a great show of gagging. Alex felt that he outdid himself in the mock-retching department, but no one at his table seemed particularly appreciative. Marcia looked up from her picture, met Lizzie's eyes to exchange one disgusted glance, and then went back to her drawing. The princess was now high up in a tower, maybe waiting for a prince to come along and rescue her.

"Good, Tom," Ms. Van Winkle said. "That *used* to be the recommended treatment, but now the American Medical Association advises that you not take the risks involved in that procedure. Instead, have the victim rest; this is very important. Position the patient so that the bite is lower than the heart. And immobilize and bandage the bitten limb. You can all do that, right?"

Wrong. Alex thought back to Julius's drooping bandages of the week before. But Alex suspected that Julius would do a better job of bandaging a bitten limb than he would of sucking the venom out of it.

He should be able to think of some funny remark now. "Hey, Marcia," he might say, "I guess we won't be trying to suck the venom out of you, after all."

In the good old days, such a witty line would have earned him a playful swat from Marcia, and then he would have tried to tickle her, and they would both have ended up doing time-out in the hall together.

But as he watched her drawing a princess without any prince, her pretty head bent low over her notebook, he knew he wouldn't have the nerve to say it. If only he could tell her, "Guess what, I think your hair looks great today, and your zit hardly shows at all anymore, and I like your picture of the princess in the tower, and I *am* the one who toilet-papered your tree."

But, thanks to his dad, he couldn't say a word of it.

7

" 'ONE PAIR OF WATERPROOF SNOW PANTS,' " Alex's mother read from the outdoor ed REQUIRED SUPPLIES list, on Saturday morning.

"It's not going to snow in late May," Alex protested.

"It certainly can snow in May up in the high country where you're going. Besides, the list says 'one pair of waterproof snow pants.' We have to follow the list."

Alex retrieved the snow pants from the back of his closet. They were too short, after his winter growth spurt. He sure hoped it didn't snow enough for him to have to wear them. The short pants would look like a costume for *Dance of the Dork*. The title pleased him. The next time Julius did something klutzy, he could say, "Hey, are you auditioning for *Dance of the Dork*?"

"Here they are." Alex threw them on the mounting pile of clothes on the floor next to his duffel.

" 'One heavy-weight jacket or parka.' "

Why hadn't his mother told him to get his parka when she sent him to get his snow pants? Alex felt like a golden retriever, trotting back and forth from duffel to closet to fetch whatever his mother wanted.

"Is there anything else we need from the closet while I'm there?"

"It's easier to check things off one at a time," his mother said. "We don't want to get confused and forget anything."

Grumbling under his breath, Alex fetched his parka. Next, she'd probably send him for waterproof mittens—first for the left mitten, then for the right.

" 'One pair of waterproof mittens.' "

At least he could bring both mittens in one trip. Defying his mother's system, he brought his woolen hat back with him, too.

" 'One warm winter hat.' "

"Ta-dah!" He held it out to her with a grin, and, with a grin, she put another check mark on the list.

His father appeared in the family room. "What the heck is all this? He's going for three nights to a ranch, not for six years to Outer Mongolia."

Alex's mother waved the list at him. He came over to inspect it himself. " 'One travel-sized toothpaste. One toothbrush.' One toothbrush? If our seventh graders need to be told to bring a toothbrush to outdoor ed, the state of public education in this district is even worse than I think it is."

"Honey, we're not finished yet," Alex's mother said mildly, holding out her hand for the list.

"I'm not finished yet, either. 'One nine-by-eleven spiral notebook.' I'm sure the size of the notebook is very important. 'One set of twelve colored pencils.' Twelve? What's wrong with twenty-four? And what are you going to be *coloring* up there, anyway? Hello? Folks, these are seventh graders! Haven't they moved on from coloring?"

"It's for our nature journals," Alex said, though why he should want to defend the list he didn't know. "In case we want to draw wildflowers or something."

"That's right. The nature journals. I had almost forgotten about the nature journals. 'What Nature Means to Me,' or 'Why Kids Today Can't Do Long Division Without a Calculator.' Wait. Listen to this. Oh, this is rich. 'One small stuffed animal (optional).' The small stuffed animal is optional. Alex, how big would you say Mr. Bear is? They don't give the dimensions for *small* here. Less than eight inches tall?"

"I'm not taking him!"

"Al, honey, we really do need to finish up here. Cara and Dax are going to be here any minute for lunch, and I don't have anything ready yet, and—"

"Let Lover Boy fix his own sandwich. Isn't that what they teach them in vo-tech? *First* you spread the peanut butter, *then* you spread the jelly." But he relinquished the list to Alex's mother.

"Where were we?" she asked Alex.

"I don't remember."

"Oh," Alex's father called back in parting, "pack for me, too, will you, hon? But skip the colored pencils. And the teddy bear."

He winked at Alex as he left the room, as if the two of them had been making fun of the list together. But it hadn't felt that way to Alex. His father had been making fun of *his* school, *his* teachers, *his* bear. Alex was about ready to get rid of Mr. Bear, anyway. It wasn't worth all this grief to keep him.

"He didn't mean it that way," his mother said gently.

"It's like, he can't even go an hour without picking on me or Cara about something."

"That's just how he is."

Alex had to ask her. "Would *you* want him going on outdoor ed with *you* if you were me?"

His mother hesitated. He could tell she was torn between wanting to be loyal to her husband and honest with her son.

"Would you?"

"I'd be glad that he *wanted* to go, that he cared enough to go."

"But would you be glad that he was *going*?"

His mother pulled the zipper shut on his duffel. "No," she said quietly. "I don't think I would."

Alex was dreading lunch. Hearing his father say sarcastic things *about* Dax was bad enough. Hearing him say sarcastic things *to* Dax would be even worse. But his father must have had enough fun with the outdoor ed supplies list, because he took his plate upstairs to his computer, and the rest of the family ate in peace.

"So we have Alex all packed for outdoor ed," his mother said when they were seated at the table.

"How come they start all these fun programs exactly one year after I'm too old to do any of them?" Cara asked. "The year after I left elementary school, they started putting on those great fifth-grade plays, remember? And the year I hit eighth grade, they started seventh-grade outdoor ed."

"Makes you wonder, doesn't it," Dax teased. But his teasing had no edge to it. He had one arm draped around Cara's shoulders as he ate with the other, occasionally feeding Cara a grape or potato chip.

"Maybe they'll *stop* having outdoor ed the year after *I* go on it," Alex said, only half joking. Maybe he and Dave could think of something to do at outdoor ed that would change the course of West Creek Middle School history forever.

"You mean, the year after *Dad* goes on it," Cara corrected.

Alex shot his sister a grateful look.

"Come on, you two," their mother said, her usual cheerful, positive tone back again. "Outdoor ed is going to be a great experience for Alex. I don't think you children appreciate all the opportunities you have nowadays."

"I do," Cara said dreamily, leaning back against Dax's encircling arm.

This was definitely getting too mushy. "Hey," Alex said to Dax, "my English teacher gave us some of that book you were talking about, to read in class."

"Amazing stuff, isn't it?"

"Uh-huh," Alex said, even though he hadn't really read it. He thought again of his own journal: *Animal Droppings I Have Stepped In*. If his dad was coming to outdoor ed, he had to think of some way-cool plan for surviving it. He just had to.

Dave came over after lunch. He did a double take when he saw Alex's overstuffed duffel by the front door.

"You're already packed? My mom packs everything the night before. The *hour* before. We aren't leaving until *Tuesday*, man."

"My mom likes to do everything far ahead. She says it makes for less stress."

Dave gave the duffel an admiring kick. "What have you got in here, rocks?"

"Just the stuff on the list."

"What list?"

"They sent home a list. With all kinds of stuff on it. 'One pair of snow pants. One flashlight. One comb.' Didn't you get it?"

"Oh, that list. I don't think I ever brought it home. It's probably still in my locker somewhere."

Alex shook his head, grinning. Dave's family was definitely different from his. If there was a bake sale at school, his own mother brought a made-from-scratch cake; Ethan's mother brought a made-from-a-mix cake; Julius's mother brought a store-bought cake; Dave's mother didn't bring a cake at all, because Dave had never taken home the notice about the bake sale.

Even if he had, Mrs. Barnett might not have bothered. She was a single mother and too busy with her job and three kids to do PTO stuff. Dave's dad had left before Dave started kindergarten. Sometimes Alex secretly envied Dave. Alex always had a restful time at his friend's messy, disorganized house, with dirty dishes and heaps of unfolded laundry everywhere.

"I rode past Faitak's house on my way over here," Dave said. "It looks like someone T.P.ed one of her trees. There was some toilet paper way up high, like her parents couldn't get it down."

Alex tried to force his face into an expression of bland innocence, though all week long he had been dying to tell Dave about last weekend's adventure.

"Does she have any brothers or sisters?" Dave asked.

"Yeah, a sister, a half sister, who mainly lives somewhere else."

"So who did it? Do you think it was neighborhood kids? I think it had to be one of us."

Alex felt the bland innocence on his face giving way to sly pride. He couldn't help it. He wasn't a professional actor; he was a seventh-grade kid.

"*You* did it?"

Alex put his finger to his lips in an exaggerated gesture of secrecy. "My lips are sealed."

"You and who else? Winfield and Zimmerman?"

"When your grandma was here. I called you, remember?"

"Aw, man." Dave whimpered in disappointment. "Does she know?"

"No! And you can't tell her. Swear you won't tell."

Dave looked puzzled; Alex didn't blame him. What was the point of wrapping a person's entire tree with toilet paper if you couldn't even take credit for it afterward? For the second time in three minutes, he felt a quick, shameful surge of jealousy because Dave didn't have a dad.

"Okay. Whatever you say."

Partly to avoid saying anything more about Marcia's tree, Alex turned back to the original topic of conversation. "Outdoor ed. What's the plan?"

"The plan?" Then Dave smiled. "Oh, the *plan*."

"Three nights," Alex said thoughtfully. "Three nocturnal disturbances?"

"Three what?"

The expression was Alex's dad's. When Alex was little and had bad dreams and came to find his mother, his father always grumbled the next morning about "nocturnal disturbances." One thing Alex had learned was that sarcasm often involved saying regular things in dressed-up words. Over the years it had been very good for his vocabulary.

"*Nocturnal* means 'nighttime.' *Disturbances* means 'disturbances.' "

"I like it." Dave's voice was mellow with appreciation. "What kind of disturbances?"

"Well, I don't think we can plan the whole thing ahead of time. We'll have to scope out some of it when we get there. But wait—" Even as Alex was stalling to think of the perfect idea, the perfect idea came to him. "I'll be right back."

He tore up to his room and down again. "Close your eyes."

Dave looked apprehensive, but he closed his eyes tight. Standing a few feet away from Dave, Alex slowly shook his real, genuine rattlesnake rattle.

Dave didn't react. The soft dry rattle didn't sound like much, not when you were sitting in someone's family room.

"Think dusty trails," Alex said in a low, hypnotic

voice. "Think of thick underbrush, hidden danger." He shook the rattle again, harder this time. "Think of bare ankles, exposed to venomous fangs . . ."

Dave's eyes flew open. "Snakes? Rattlesnakes?"

Alex held out the rattle for Dave's inspection. "It has possibilities, no?"

To the outdoor ed REQUIRED SUPPLIES list he added in his mind: one real rattlesnake rattle.

IT WAS COOL AND OVERCAST on Tuesday morning when Alex's mother drove Alex and his dad, with their duffels, to West Creek to board the bus. She got out of the car to give each of them a goodbye hug. Alex let her do it.

Three buses stood waiting for them. After his name was checked off, Alex boarded the first bus with Dave; his father had already boarded the rear bus with another dad. So far, so good.

On every class trip Alex had ever been on, the buses left late. As they waited, Alex took a survey of who was on their bus. Ethan and Julius were there, sitting together, of course. Lizzie was there, sitting with Alison. From the window Alex saw Marcia board the second bus with Sarah. He settled back with Dave into their rear seat, savoring the sweetness of relief.

"Did you work any more on the plan?" Dave asked.

"Nah," Alex said confidently. "It'll come."

The old-lady bus driver droned through the same safety regulations Alex had heard a million times since kindergarten. Then she started up the engine and eased out of the West Creek parking lot. Outdoor ed had begun.

Some of the girls tried to start a sing-along. Alex and Dave ignored them. The singers gave up soon afterward. It was going to be almost a three-hour drive to Elliot Ranch. Even the girls wouldn't be able to stand that much singing.

The road became narrow and twisting. Alex hoped the bus driver knew what she was doing. He'd be willing to bet that his father was sitting right behind the driver on his bus, giving him or her pointers on mountain driving.

Maybe the old-lady bus driver *could* have used a few tips. Alex's stomach began to feel a bit queasy. He didn't think he was going to be sick, but he wished he had some fresh air on his face. His forehead felt damp and clammy. He tried to open his window, but it was sealed shut.

He had his first inspiration of the trip. "We could pretend we were going to throw up," he suggested to Dave.

Dave's eyes shone. "Both of us?"

"Too much of a coincidence."

Alex waited to see if Dave would volunteer to do the honors. After a moment's pause, Alex said graciously, "I'll do it." Leave it to Alex. And, actually, he thought he might be convincingly pale. Another lurch or two of the bus, and he might even be green.

"Okay," Alex said. "Here goes."

He stood up and started making his way down the aisle.

"No standing while the bus is in motion," the driver called out.

"I . . . think . . . I'm . . . going . . . to . . . be . . . sick."

The kids nearest to Alex screamed and leaned as far toward the windows as possible, so that the aisle kids were practically sitting on the window kids' laps. Mrs. Martin and Ms. Van Winkle both had stricken looks on their faces, as if painfully aware that they were the only teachers on the bus and in charge of averting any impending catastrophe.

The bus screeched to a halt. The door wheezed open. "Not in the bus," the driver ordered, sounding more authoritative than Alex would have given her credit for. She jerked her thumb toward the open door. "Out there."

Alex stopped at about the fourth row, by Lizzie and Alison, and swallowed mightily, as if he were about to heave.

Lizzie stood up suddenly. If Alex had felt green before, Lizzie looked fresh from the Emerald City of Oz. "I think I'm going to be sick, too," she whispered.

Alex didn't waste any more time with pantomimes. It was clear that Lizzie wasn't pretending. And if Lizzie threw up right now, he was the one she would throw up on. He hurried on out the door. Lizzie stumbled after him.

"If you're going to be sick, you two, do it and get back on the bus. We're already behind schedule," the driver called after them.

Alex didn't think much of her bedside manner. Maybe there was a reason she was a bus driver instead of a nurse.

It was a good twenty degrees chillier on the mountain pass than it had been in West Creek. The cold air in Alex's face felt good.

"Are you okay?" he asked Lizzie with genuine concern, though he was careful to stand a couple of feet away.

"I guess so. It was just that when I thought you were going to be sick . . ." The memory drained the returning color from Lizzie's face.

"Take deep breaths," Alex said, impressed by his own calm in the face of possible vomit. Ms. Van Winkle should see him now: Dr. Ryan, able administrator of first aid to the nauseated.

Lizzie took the deep breaths, and her cheeks flushed

ever so slightly pink: Dr. Ryan's first medical success story.

"Are you two done out there?" the driver yelled to them.

Alex looked at Lizzie. She nodded. "Yeah!" he yelled back.

On the bus again, Alex accepted congratulations from Dave and the other guys sitting near him. Then he tuned out and half dozed for the rest of the ride. He had done his share for the bus trip. Any further excitement was up to someone else.

They reached Elliot Ranch a little past noon. It was very windy now, and the low gray skies were threatening rain, if not snow—if not a major spring blizzard. The teachers announced that they would eat their sack lunches outdoors. "Lunch first, then mountain biking!" Coach Krubek called out heartily.

Glad to be off the bus, Alex followed the others to a group of picnic tables set in a grove of aspen and oak trees and opened his lunch. His mom packed great lunches. That day he had a thick roast-beef sandwich, homemade potato salad, huge soft ginger cookies, and lemonade.

His dad ate at a table with some of the teachers. Marcia and Sarah were at the table closest to Alex, laughing and chatting in such a jolly way that Alex felt hopeful, too. Maybe Marcia had finally forgiven him for all his stupid remarks.

To test this theory, Alex scooped up a handful of acorns from the ground and tossed one gently at Marcia's back. She gave a little scream and looked around. Alex devoted himself to his last cookie. When her back was turned again, he launched another acorn.

"Alex Ryan, stop that!"

Marcia got up and flounced over to his table. Her hair was in two short pigtails, tied with blue ribbons. She was so cute he thought that his heart might stop beating right on the spot, and that he'd keel over and die.

"Stop what?"

"You know what!" Marcia giggled, an excellent sign.

"Are you ready for mountain biking this afternoon?" Alex asked, since the conversation was going so well.

"Are you? Someone told me that you hadn't taken off your training wheels yet." Marcia giggled again. Her pigtails bounced ever so slightly in time with each giggle.

Alex tried to think of a friendly insult to top Marcia's, but after so many unfriendly insults lately, he was out of practice. "I saw you riding your bike the other day around the neighborhood," he lied. "You looked like a trained gorilla in the circus."

Oops. To Alex's dismay, Marcia's face flushed a deep, angry red. *Don't ever tease girls about their looks!* Why couldn't he remember that one simple truth, which by now should have been burned into his poor battered brain?

It was too late to turn back now. "I meant that as a compliment," he protested. "Trained gorillas are *good* bike riders."

Oh, no. That didn't help at all. At least Marcia didn't jump up and run away this time. But her eyes glistened with something close to tears.

Coach Krubek whistled for everyone's attention. "Time for mountain biking!" he bellowed in his loud coach's voice. "Line up over at that gray barn to our right, roughly by height, and we'll fit you with bikes and helmets and get you started. Helmets are required for everybody. Parents and teachers, that means you, too. The other main rule: stay with your partner, and stay on the trail. There are over a hundred miles of trails here at Elliot Ranch. We don't want to lose anybody."

"What if it rains?" someone called out.

"You should have your rain gear in your day pack," the coach said.

Great, Alex thought. There was nothing like a refreshing long bike ride on muddy trails in the pouring rain.

"What if it snows?" someone else asked.

"It's not going to snow."

Alex thought of the instructions printed on the outdoor ed REQUIRED SUPPLIES list: "Mountain weather is unpredictable. Snowstorms are common even in late spring and early summer." Apparently Coach Krubek hadn't read that far on the list.

The West Creek kids hastily cleared the lunch tables. Then everyone, except for Lizzie, fell in line for the equipment. Alex suddenly remembered that last fall, in a dumb get-acquainted game in family living, Lizzie had confessed that she didn't know how to ride a bike. It was still the strangest thing Alex had ever heard. Not knowing how to ride a bike was like not knowing how to walk or swim. There were some things that every normal twelve- or thirteen-year-old person knew how to do. Not that Lizzie was what you would call "normal."

Alex guessed that Lizzie would just stay behind with somebody's parent—not his, he hoped. Maybe Ethan would make a big show of offering to stay behind, too. Ethan was always very gallant where Lizzie was concerned.

To Alex's surprise, Marcia left the line and joined Lizzie, who was standing off on one side next to Ms. Singpurwalla. Marcia knew how to ride a bike. Was she trying to stick with Lizzie? Alex hadn't thought the two girls were *that* friendly.

Curious now, Alex got out of line himself. He could ask Ms. S. where the bathroom was. That was a perfectly reasonable question.

Edging toward Ms. S., he heard Marcia say, "I don't think I can ride a bike today."

"Why not?"

"I hurt my ankle."

"When? Just now?"

Marcia looked flustered. "Yesterday. When I was roller-skating."

Now it was Ms. S.'s turn to look flustered. "Do you have a note? What about the hike tomorrow? We're going to be doing a *lot* of hiking. Did your parents have a doctor look at it?"

"I'm sure it will be fine tomorrow for the hike," Marcia said desperately. "It just hurts if I pedal a bike."

Ms. S. looked unconvinced, but didn't send Marcia back to the line again. "Alex. What do you want?"

"Um—where's the bathroom?"

"We'll all stop at the rest room before we head out on the trails."

As he returned to the line, he saw Marcia whisper something to Lizzie. Lizzie put her arm around Marcia's shoulders. Then Lizzie, usually so sweet and shy, gave Alex a furious glare.

So Marcia wasn't going mountain biking because Alex had said she looked like a gorilla when she was biking? Now what was he supposed to say?

Alex gave up. The more he tried, the worse things got. Lately, it was the story of his life.

Out on the trail, Alex managed to forget his latest run-in with Marcia. The clouds that had seemed so threatening had lifted, and the sunshine was warm on his back and shoulders. Alex loved bike riding almost as much as he loved running.

His dad chose to go mountain biking, too, though most of the parents and teachers had stayed behind at the lodge, leaving the kids to the supervision of the ranch's trained guides. Passing Alex and Dave on an open part of the trail, his dad flashed them a grin. "Forget the law firm!" he called to Alex. "This is the life!"

His dad looked good on his bike. He didn't have a bulgy stomach, like Julius's dad, or a receding hairline, like Ethan's. For a fleeting moment Alex felt proud of his dad for being cooler than the other dads. Smarter and more successful, too. His dad was the only one who was a hot-shot lawyer. Ethan's dad cleaned carpets for a living; Julius's dad was some kind of boring accountant. And Dave, of course, didn't have a dad at all.

"Come on, you two!" his dad yelled back over his shoulder. "Don't wuss out on me!"

The moment faded. Alex was torn between pedaling harder, to try to keep up, and just admitting defeat. He chose defeat.

When the mountain-biking excursion was over, Alex felt tired and sore, but in a good way. Now they had free time for the hour before dinner, to settle into their rooms, shower, play some pool or Ping-Pong in the lodge rec room.

"This would be a good time to take a short walk and get started on your nature journals," Ms. S. suggested. Alex knew that exactly one person would take her up on that idea: Lizzie Archer. Though perhaps Lizzie had already crammed her journal full of poems while everyone else had been out biking. Unless she had spent the whole time talking with Marcia about how terrible Alex was.

Alex was sharing his room with Dave and two guys he didn't know very well. You were guaranteed one friend from your request list; for the rest, you had to put up with whomever you got. But his other two roommates weren't bad.

He took a long shower. The water felt good on his

aching muscles. Then he and Dave shot some pool until it was time to eat. Although dinner was served cafeteria style, the food was several notches above the West Creek Middle School fare. Alex went back for seconds on the barbecued pork, baked beans, home-style fries, and apple cobbler. He even felt cheerful enough to speak to his dad when they met at the bussing station with their trays.

"Don't tell Mom how good the food was," he said.

"We want to keep her on her toes, don't we?" his dad replied. "Maybe we can get the cobbler recipe from the chef before we go."

"And the barbecue recipe, too."

His dad gave him a wink, and they both smacked their lips.

The first after-dinner activity was watching an educational program about Colorado wildlife on the ranch's large-screen TV. When it was over, the girls' P.E. teacher turned on the lights, to reveal that at least half the kids had fallen fast asleep during the video. Alex had dozed off himself in a couple of places.

"All right," Coach Rorty blared, as if speaking through an invisible megaphone. "Our main activity this evening is going to be—square dancing! Elliot Ranch has an experienced caller, fiddler, and teacher who's going to teach us all we need to know. Mr. Dee, it's all yours."

The kids who were fully awake emitted loud, heart-rending groans. Those who were still half-asleep blinked their eyes in dazed confusion. Alex was sorry now that he hadn't paid more attention during the outdoor ed information night so he could have been psychologically prepared for the horror of square dancing. Then again, maybe it was better not to have known.

"Come on, kids, it's not going to be so bad," Mr. Dee said with a big grin. He had a down-home, folksy way of talking, which went with his bib overalls, plaid flannel shirt, and bushy red-and-gray beard. It wasn't going to be so bad for *him* maybe. Though any job that required bib overalls looked pretty bad to Alex.

As he continued talking at a steady clip, Mr. Dee started playing his fiddle. He could definitely play, bib overalls or no bib overalls.

"All right, ladies to my right, gents to my left; that's right; gents, go find yourselves a lady; there's some mighty purty gals here; come on, fellas, don't be bashful; ladies, help 'em out, give 'em a big smile; gents, they aren't going to bite you; come on, gents, who's going to be your lucky lady tonight?"

No one, apparently. None of the boys moved forward out of the tight, desperate knot they had formed in front of the lodge's enormous stone fireplace.

Coach Krubek walked toward them, with quiet menace in his approach. The fiddle music continued, but Mr. Dee for the moment had dropped his patter, evidently preferring to let the West Creek teachers try their own methods of persuasion.

"Boys," Coach Krubek said, "this is a square dance. You are all going to dance. Dancing is not optional. Dancing is mandatory. Go. Now. Dance."

For extra effect, he pulled a pad of West Creek Middle School Behavior Modification Slips from his shirt pocket and thumbed through it thoughtfully.

One boy—braver than the rest? or more cowardly?—gave in and walked across the dance floor to where the girls were clustered and glaring at the boys for their stalling. Others followed. Alex watched as Ethan asked a girl from their math class, Julius asked a quiet girl who sat next to him in English class, Tom asked Lizzie. Even Dave inched his way across the room, toward Marcia's friend Sarah.

Alex still stood rooted in place. To ask Marcia or not to ask Marcia, that was the question. At the last seventh-grade dance, back in March, Alex had asked Marcia twice for boys' choices, and she had asked him three times for girls' choices, including both slow dances of the evening. He knew girls thought it was a big thing to ask a guy for a slow dance. But that seemed so long ago.

On the one hand, if he asked her, she might refuse, though maybe Coach Rorty had given the girls the same speech Coach Krubek had given the boys, that dancing wasn't optional. She might have pads of West Creek Middle School Behavior Modification Slips, too. But it would be pretty bad to have a girl dance with you just because she'd get a Behavior Modification Slip if she didn't.

On the other hand, if he didn't ask her, she might hate him for life. Of course, she already hated him for life. But girls seemed somehow capable of hating you for more than one lifetime.

As Alex remained paralyzed with indecision, another boy, Spencer, asked Marcia. Would she now hate him for life because he hadn't beaten the competition for her hand? Alex couldn't think about that now. He slunk up to one of the only three girls who were left, a very tall, skinny girl named Tanya. He couldn't quite get out the question *May I have this dance?* but she seemed to understand his grudging intent and, looking as unenthusiastic as he felt, followed him out to the floor.

Mr. Dee, fiddle still in hand, bustled about, organizing them into squares of four couples apiece. Alex and Tanya were put in the same square as Marcia and Spencer. Alex suddenly remembered something about square dancing: in square dancing, you changed partners all the time. So he'd get Marcia, anyway. Ms. Singpurwalla had told them about these old Greek plays, where whatever the hero tries to do, however hard he fights against it, he always ends up with his inescapable destiny. Apparently, Alex's inescapable destiny was Marcia.

Marcia pretended that Alex wasn't there. Alex pretended that Marcia wasn't there. He wished he could pretend that Tanya wasn't there. She towered over him, so that Alex knew he looked small and silly beside her, even though he was one of the taller seventh-grade boys. Across the room he could see his dad, grinning in his direction.

Mr. Dee resumed his place by the microphone. "This first dance is called the Turkey Trot. I'll walk you through it slowly the first time. Then we'll let 'er fly. Gents, bow to your ladies. Ladies, curtsy to your gents."

If anything looked dumber than girls curtsying while wearing jeans, Alex didn't know what it was. Except maybe a boy bowing to a girl who was half a head taller than he was.

"Now swing your partner. Link your right arms and swing around once." Reluctantly Alex linked arms with Tanya. It was little comfort that she seemed to hate dancing with him every bit as much as he hated dancing with her.

"Now grand right and left. That means you move in a circle, gents in one direction, ladies in the other, holding out first your right hand, then your left, so that you shake hands with every lady or gent that you pass."

Great confusion ensued as several people forgot which hand was which. Glancing at the square next to theirs, Alex saw that Julius had already managed to trip one of the girls he was trying to shake hands with, and they had both gone sprawling. When Ms. Van Winkle told them they might need their first-aid skills at outdoor ed, she must have been thinking about the square dancing.

As Alex passed Marcia in the grand right and left, their hands touched so briefly that neither of them made a big deal out of it. When he had to swing her, he just swung her, unlike some of the boys, who whirled their partners as hard as if they were playing crack-the-whip on the playground.

The run-through was bad enough; the actual dance, at full speed, with Mr. Dee's comments coming in a constant, unintelligible stream, was almost impossible. But the crazy, frenzied pace of it got people laughing. The collisions, which at first had seemed embarrassing, now seemed hilarious. And at full speed the dance was over more quickly.

They danced three more dances with the same partners, in the same squares. Then Mr. Dee sent them back to their corners again, girls on one side, boys on the other.

"Ladies, it's your turn now. That's right, ladies, go get 'em!"

No waving of Behavior Modification Slips was

needed this time. The girls obediently started across the room toward the boys.

Alex knew Marcia wouldn't ask him, because he hadn't asked her. Sure enough, Marcia asked Dave. He knew she had chosen Dave deliberately, because he and Dave were standing right next to each other. Marcia didn't want Alex to miss seeing her flagrantly choosing someone else.

He hoped Tanya wouldn't choose him. Toward the end of the previous dance, she had been acting suspiciously friendly, laughing too hard when he swung her around, giggling for no discernable reason. He had nothing against Tanya, but he had had enough of dancing with someone twice his size. But Tanya didn't ask him. She asked Julius, even though Julius was easily the worst dancer in the seventh grade.

Maybe Lizzie would ask him. He knew she liked him well enough; she had forgiven him for his relentless teasing over the years. But Lizzie asked Ethan.

The group of remaining boys was fast dwindling. Alex felt a strange surge of panic. Worse than having to square-dance with a girl would be not even being picked to square-dance with a girl. Alex wasn't the type not to get picked for things. He was always one of the first kids called when they were choosing sides for games; at all three seventh-grade dances he had never had to worry about having a partner for every dance.

But with Marcia turned against him, and turning all her friends against him, even Lizzie . . .

Out on the dance floor the squares were already forming, the giggles were already being giggled. Two boys were left now—Alex and a short fat boy with funny clothes, named Henry.

Only one girl was left, a short fat girl with funny clothes, named Randi. Alex hadn't realized there was one boy too many. He hadn't noticed who was left over during the last set of dances, or what had happened to him. Alex had been part of the dancing and giggling then.

Randi hesitated, evidently going through her own version of eeny, meeny, miny, mo. Alex stared down at his worn-out tennis shoes, unwilling to beg with his eyes. When he looked up, Randi and Henry were heading for the dance floor together. Alex was all alone.

Alone for one brief moment. His social studies teacher, Mrs. Martin, was bearing down on him. If Alex had to be the recipient of a teacher's pity, why couldn't it have been Ms. Singpurwalla? Mrs. Martin was probably fifty, every bit as tall as Tanya, and a good hundred and fifty pounds heavier. "May I have this dance?" she asked him kindly.

Alex didn't need a Behavior Modification Slip waved in his face to know that this was an offer he couldn't refuse.

As he trailed behind Mrs. Martin to the last incomplete square, the square of leftovers, the square of losers, he had to walk past where his father was standing with two other dads. His father, motioning in his direction, said something to the others. Apparently it was something funny, because all three fathers laughed.

10

ALEX WAS GRATEFUL THAT DAVE made only one crack to him about square-dancing with Mrs. Martin. As they walked back to their room that night, Dave used an Auntie Em voice from *The Wizard of Oz* and babbled, "Dorothy, oh, where are you, Dorothy?" Mrs. Martin's first name was Dorothy. Alex swatted him, Dave grinned, and that was that. Alex's new definition of a true friend was "someone who makes only one wisecrack following the most humiliating experience of your life."

At breakfast the next morning, as Alex had dreaded, his father was less restrained. When they met at the orange juice machine, his father said, "Square-dancing muscles sore, eh?"

"Aw, Dad," Alex said.

His father chuckled. "Tall women have their appeal." A double crack: his dad had obviously seen him dancing first with Tanya, then with Mrs. Martin.

Two people were ahead of them in the orange juice line. Alex was sorry now that he had ever wanted orange juice, but retreat at this point was impossible. Alex would only lower himself further in his dad's opinion if he acted as if he couldn't take some teasing.

"Mom's not tall," he said, to say something.

"Well, I know how to pick 'em. Why you and Cara . . ." His father trailed off.

Alex knew that it pained his dad to have his daughter choose someone like Dax and to have his son suddenly so unpopular as to be chosen by nobody. Marcia was the kind of square-dancing partner his father would have approved of—cute, pretty, lively personality, always surrounded by a chattering group of other popular girls.

It was finally Alex's turn for the juice machine. He filled his glass halfway full.

"Drink up," his father said, his jovial tone restored. "Gotta catch up with those dance partners of yours."

Ha. What would his dad do if Alex said, *Stop it, it's not funny. Do you think I liked being humiliated like that in front of everybody, in front of Dave and the other guys, in front of Marcia, in front of you?*

Instead he forced a laugh and carried his tray back to the table.

It was the day of the big hike. They were going to hike

all day, nature journals and soil-sampling kits in their day packs, to a set of cabins at the far end of the ranch. They'd spend the night there, cooking their own dinner, which Alex suspected would be a far cry from the barbecue provided by the ranch chefs last night. Then they'd hike back on a different set of trails tomorrow.

A ranch truck was going to meet them at the cabin with their groceries, sleeping bags, and other supplies. When this had been explained the night before, Marcia had asked, "If we can drive there, why are we going to walk there?" None of the teachers had answered.

As they stood now in front of the lodge, shouldering their heavy day packs, the first raindrops started falling.

"Get out your rain ponchos," Coach Krubek ordered.

"I can't believe this," Dave said to Alex. He began rummaging through his backpack, getting all his other gear soaked in the process. "It never rains in the morning in Colorado."

"It's raining now," Alex said.

In their ponchos, the students looked like a flock of wet birds. It was hard to tell one bird from another, except for the very small birds, like Lizzie, and the very large birds, like Tanya. And the very clumsy birds, like Julius, who was still struggling to find the head hole in his poncho and maneuver it into the vicinity of his head.

Alex looked around warily to see which bird was Marcia. He strolled casually over to the other side of the group, as if he was just stretching his leg muscles while they waited. On his way, he passed Lizzie. Her small, freckled face was alive with happiness.

"Don't you just love the rain?" she asked.

Alex was so relieved that one of the girls was actually speaking to him that he said, "Sure. Yeah. It's so . . . wet."

Lizzie laughed. "Smell."

Alex wrinkled up his nose obligingly. He didn't smell much of anything. "You haven't seen Marcia, have you?" he asked.

Lizzie's face changed, as if she was remembering that she was mad at Alex on Marcia's behalf. "She's over there. In the lime green poncho."

Should Alex try to approach her? The lime green of Marcia's poncho was electric in its brightness, like a neon sign flashing DANGER. Maybe he'd better not.

"Thanks." Alex matched the coolness of his tone to Lizzie's.

The hikers set off. The trails were muddy already. Some of the kids tried to scramble through the underbrush on the sides of the trail, to avoid getting their boots all covered with mud.

"Stay on the trail," Coach Krubek called out. "A little mud won't hurt you. But a hundred pairs of tramping feet walking off the trail can cause environmental damage that takes years to repair. Besides, you want to see where you're walking. Walk in the brush, you could be walking into ticks. Or rattlesnakes."

The last word did the trick. Those who had tuned out to the remarks about damage to the environment now sprang back onto the trail with terrified shrieks. Alex slipped his hand into his pocket and closed his fingers around his rattlesnake rattle. Maybe he shouldn't use it, after all. But if he didn't have *any* plan, then he'd just be the guy nobody wanted to dance with, the butt of his father's unfunny jokes.

They walked slowly and steadily for about an hour, all uphill, a fairly gradual ascent, but steep enough that Alex was starting to feel sweaty and winded when they stopped under the shelter of some pine trees for a break.

"Drink lots of water," Coach Krubek said.

"Did any of you see anything to write about in your nature journals?" Ms. S. asked. Even in a rain poncho, she looked beautiful. Raindrops glistened in the dark hair framing her dusky face.

Alex pulled out his journal, just to impress her, and tried to think of something to write.

Ode to Rain

The rain
Is a pain.
Wet trails make me slip.
Drip, drip, drip, drip.

That was all he could think of. Next to him Lizzie was settled on a damp log, scribbling away.

"What are you writing about?" he asked, taking another chance at friendliness.

"The rain. Do you think it looks like liquid silver, spilling from the leaden goblet of the skies?"

"Definitely," Alex said.

"What are you writing about?"

"Same thing. I haven't gotten too far." He read to her what he had written. To his relief, she laughed. He hadn't entirely lost his touch.

As soon as Lizzie laughed, an electric lime green bird materialized beside her. "Lizzie," the bird said warningly. Alex wondered if Marcia had written anything in her journal yet. He could imagine a poem or two:

Ode to Alex Ryan

I hate you, Alex Ryan.
I hate you all day long.
Everything you say is dumb.
Everything you do is wrong.

He turned back to his poem about the rain, but he couldn't think of anything else to add. Maybe it was perfect just the way it was.

By the next break, for lunch and soil sampling beside a spring-swollen creek, the rain had stopped and the sun was fighting to break through the clearing clouds. Julius lost his footing on the creek bank and soaked one leg up to the knee. Hopping about, trying to dry it, he almost took a second tumble. Ethan caught him just in time.

The hikers had their ponchos off now and stuffed in their day packs. Without her bright green covering, Marcia looked less alarming, more like a regular girl. She had a bandanna tied around her dark hair that was even cuter than her pigtails had been yesterday. Did Alex dare say something to her about it?

"Nice bandanna," he said, swinging his pack on after the soil sampling.

Marcia stared at him, once again, with unmistakable rage. What, he wondered, could have been so offensive about "nice bandanna"?

"You know I'm only wearing this because I ran out of hot water partway through my shower this morning, so I didn't get to wash my hair. But leave it to you, Alex Ryan. The worse someone feels, the worse you try to make them feel."

Alex couldn't let the unfairness of this accusation pass by. "But it does look nice. I meant it. It's cute."

"Cute like a hillbilly in a cartoon, maybe."

Alex gave up. Apparently Marcia really thought she looked awful in her scarf. If even sincere compliments could make a girl mad, then there was no hope for any boy, ever.

"Forget it," Alex said. "Forget I said anything."

Marcia gave a short, shaky laugh. "Now you want me to forget it. Let me tell you something. People don't forget things. I don't forget things. I never forget things."

Alex turned and walked away.

Dave fell into step beside him as they continued up the trail. "Did you bring it?"

"Bring what?" Alex asked gloomily.

"*It.*"

"Yeah, I brought it."

"And?"

Alex didn't reply. *Nice bandanna.* Who would have believed that those were words so terrible they could never be forgiven or forgotten? Of course, Marcia wouldn't have reacted that way to this particular remark if it hadn't been for earlier remarks about zits, used toilet paper, and gorillas.

His father, side by side with Coach Krubek, passed the boys. Leave it to his dad to attach himself to the teacher whose good opinion Alex most valued.

"Come on, Alex," his dad said. "Pick up the pace. This is a hike, not a Sunday stroll to show off your Easter bonnet."

The coach chuckled. So much for his good opinion of Alex.

"We have at least another three hours on the hike, I

think," Dave said, once the adults were out of hearing. "Three . . . long . . . dull . . . empty . . . hours."

"All right," Alex said. If there was ever a day for a plan, this was it. He made his voice low and dramatic. "We need to wait for a window of opportunity."

"What if there isn't any?"

"There will be. What do they say? 'Luck favors the prepared mind.' Something like that. We're prepared. We'll be lucky. Trust me."

After they had trudged for another forty-five minutes in the ever-hotter sun, Alex looked around and didn't see Marcia's "nice bandanna" anywhere.

"Where's Faitak?" he asked Dave.

"I haven't seen her for a while. You think she's up ahead?"

"No." Marcia was hardly an eager hiker. She was one of the seventh grade's most reliable complainers when serious physical exertion was involved. "I think she's fallen behind."

"Is this the window?"

"It's the window."

Alex led Dave off the trail. They crouched behind a cluster of juniper bushes. After about five minutes of waiting, while a few other groups of slower hikers passed them, Dave said, "Are you sure she's not up ahead?"

"Pretty sure."

They waited some more. Then Alex heard girls' voices approaching. He listened more closely. It was Lizzie and Marcia. Marcia's best friend, Sarah, who loved to hike, had long since left her behind on the trail.

"This is ridiculous," he heard Marcia say. "We've been walking for *hours*. This isn't outdoor *ed*. It's outdoor *torture*."

"Do you want to take another rest?" Lizzie asked patiently. "I think the others are pretty far ahead."

For answer, Marcia plopped down on a large rock a few feet from Alex. The window of opportunity opened wider. Alex motioned to Dave to stay quiet. He willed himself not to breathe.

"My boots are killing me," Marcia moaned.

"We could write for a while in our journals," Lizzie suggested.

"*You* could write for a while in *your* journal. I haven't seen any wildlife at all today. Except birds. If you count birds. And bugs. If you count bugs. Not that I want to see any. Do you think there are really snakes around here, or did they just say that to make us stay on their stupid muddy trail?"

If Alex lived to be a hundred and six, he would never have a window of opportunity opened wider than this one. From his pocket he retrieved the rattle. He shook it. Then he paused, to let it take effect.

Peering through the bushes, Alex could see Lizzie

freeze. More alert than Marcia, she had heard the rattle first. "Wait," Lizzie said softly.

"What?"

"I thought I heard something, but I don't hear it now."

Alex shook the rattle again, louder this time.

"I think it's a rattlesnake." Lizzie's voice was trembling.

"What should we do?" Marcia's voice rose hysterically. "Is this like the mountain lion, where you make yourself look bigger, or like the bear, where you make yourself look smaller?"

Alex gave the rattle another good shake. He made a rustling noise with his foot in the underbrush.

"Run!" Marcia shrieked.

In her terror, she bolted, not up the trail toward the others, but back down the trail the way they had come. Joining her screams to Marcia's, Lizzie pelted after her.

Alex and Dave burst out laughing. Dave was almost laughing too hard to give Alex his high five. Never had a prank been executed more perfectly. This could go in *The Guinness Book of World Records* for most flawless practical joke in the history of the world.

"We'd better go after them," Alex said when they were temporarily laughed out. "I hope they don't run all the way back to the ranch."

Smothering a new wave of laughter, the boys hurried

down the trail toward the girls. Then they stopped abruptly.

Marcia was lying sprawled in the dirt, one foot twisted grotesquely, her face contorted with pain. Lizzie had Marcia's head cradled in her lap; Lizzie's face was pale with fright and wet with tears.

"I'm so glad you're here!" Lizzie cried out when she saw Alex and Dave. "We heard a snake, and we ran. Marcia tripped on a rock, and I think she's broken her ankle, or her foot, or her leg. Broken *something*."

Marcia's eyes were closed. She was paler than Lizzie, which was saying a lot. Alex stared down at her. She wasn't going to *die*, was she? Could you die of shock brought on by a broken ankle? Because if Marcia died there on the trail at outdoor ed, it would be his fault. He, Alex Ryan, would be a murderer.

11

ALEX PULLED HIMSELF TOGETHER. Marcia was not dead or anywhere close to dying. Her ankle probably wasn't broken. People thought they had broken bones all the time, and then it turned out to be nothing but a sprain. Or not even a sprain. If he hadn't broken his arm after his twenty-foot fall from Marcia's tree, Marcia couldn't have broken her ankle tripping over one little rock on a practically smooth trail.

He looked at Dave and shook his head slightly. He hoped Dave had the sense not to say anything about the true identity of the rattlesnake.

Then he looked back at Marcia. Her ankle certainly looked bad. It was twisted in such a strange way. Alex had never seen a normal ankle twisted like that.

First aid. He couldn't believe he was actually going to use his first-aid training, after all. What *had* he learned in first aid? Something about ripping up your underwear to make bandages . . . Alex forced himself to focus. He was a good student, even if he was also a smart-aleck. He could handle this.

"Okay," Alex said, trying to sound more confident than he felt. "There's no bleeding anywhere, right?"

"Her knees and hands are skinned, but they're not really bleeding," Lizzie reported. She looked relieved to have someone else taking charge.

"Okay," Alex said again. "Shock. We need to prevent shock. She's lying down. That's good." Of course, she probably couldn't stand up. "We need to—um—loosen any tight clothing."

Lizzie checked and said, "I don't think she's wearing anything tight."

"We need to cover her with something." From his pack he pulled out a sweatshirt and spread it over Marcia's shoulders and chest, like a blanket. So far Marcia hadn't reacted to anything he had said or done. He was sure she wasn't still giving him the silent treatment, so he knew she was really in pain.

He knelt down to examine Marcia's ankle. He was a bit vague on how you were supposed to know if it was broken or not. What you *weren't* supposed to do was jerk it first this way, then that, and see if the person screamed, or if any of her bones suddenly popped through the skin. When in doubt, you were supposed to leave it alone.

A phrase came back to him from their first-aid class. "Immobilize the joint. We should immobilize the joint."

"That's right," Lizzie said. "What should we use for a splint and a bandage?"

Alex turned to Dave, to see if he agreed with their plan for treatment. Dave, staring down at Marcia's twisted ankle, was starting to turn as pale as the girls had been before. Great. Dave was going to be one of those big, hulking guys who keel over at a drop of blood or an oddly positioned ankle.

"You're not looking so hot yourself," Alex said to Dave. "You'd better sit down."

Dave dropped onto the ground. "Her ankle looks bad," he said hoarsely.

Thank you, Dr. Barnett! "Yeah, that's why we're going to bandage it."

But were they supposed to bandage it all crooked like that? Or try to stretch it out first? Alex was pretty sure they were supposed to bandage it exactly the way it was.

Since Lizzie was still holding Marcia's head, and Dave was turning out to be utterly useless, Alex looked around for a splint. He found a couple of broken tree branches that would have to do. They were fairly straight and smooth, and about the right length.

"Now we need a bandage," he said to Lizzie.

"The bandanna?" Lizzie carefully slipped it off Marcia's hair and handed it to Alex. "I have one in my pack, too." She gestured toward where it was lying by the side of the trail.

Alex opened Lizzie's neatly organized backpack and found her bandanna. He did the best he could, wrapping both bandannas around the injured ankle. Afraid of getting them too tight, he probably wasn't getting them tight enough.

"Does that feel okay?" he asked.

For answer, Marcia gave a low moan of pain. Alex didn't think she was moaning because of the bandage, though. The bandage looked pretty good.

"We're almost done, madam," Alex said gently, hoping she might smile. She didn't.

"Now what?" Lizzie asked when Alex stood up to survey his handiwork.

Alex tried to think. "When you guys were screaming before, no one came running. I think they're way ahead now. Someone might notice we're missing at some point and come back for us, but that could be a *long* time from now. It could be practically dark by then. I think maybe we—Dave and I—should try to carry her."

"How?"

"We could make kind of a chair thing with our hands."

"It's still a long way to the cabins," Lizzie said.

Marcia was a small, slim girl, not all that much bigger than Lizzie, but Alex knew it would be a long haul, lugging her up the rest of the trail. And they ran the risk of jostling her broken bone—Alex was sure now that it *was* broken—in trying to pick her up for carrying. But what else could they do? The rain clouds were gathering again. And the sooner they got her to a doctor, the better. He was strong, and Dave—if he didn't faint dead away—was strong, too.

"Dave?"

"Yeah?"

"I think we have to try to carry her."

"All the way?"

"All the way."

Alex squatted down next to Marcia. "Marcia? Are you awake? Marcia?"

She was looking a little better now, less white and clammy, but her eyes were still closed. She opened them, for an instant, then closed them again.

"Marcia, listen, Dave and I are going to try to carry you. Okay?"

"Okay," she whispered.

How to get her into the "chair" was going to be another problem. Slowly, Alex eased her into a sitting position.

"You'll have to take her pack, Lizzie," he said. They'd have enough to manage without it.

"Keep your weight on your other leg," he said. With Dave and Lizzie both supporting Marcia, one on each side, Alex helped her to stand. Marcia leaned on Lizzie, who bore her weight steadfastly, as the boys crossed hands and locked them into place.

"Okay. Sit down. Come on. We're ready for you. Come on."

Marcia lowered herself into the seat. She was pretty heavy for a skinny girl, and they hadn't even started moving yet.

"Good job. Good." Alex was becoming hypnotized by his own soothing, calming voice. "It's going to be okay. It's going to be okay. Ready, Dave?"

"I guess so," Dave said uncertainly. Alex shot him a warning glance. "I mean, yeah, I'm ready."

Conscious of Marcia's arm around his shoulder, her hand clutching the fabric of his shirt for dear life, Alex started back up the trail.

An hour or so later, as Alex was deciding that it had been a big mistake to try to lug Marcia's ever-heavier weight all the way up the trail, the first flash of lightning came, ripping the dark sky in half with a jagged explosion of brightness. A deafening clap of thunder followed immediately afterward. There couldn't have been more than a full second between the two.

"It's close," Alex said, motioning to Dave to put Marcia down.

She was fully conscious now, but still silent and subdued, clearly in a great deal of pain. "What should we do?" It was the first time she had spoken since they had begun their ascent to the cabins. She spoke so softly Alex could hardly hear what she said.

"Seek shelter," Lizzie said, quoting from their first-aid instructions.

"There isn't any shelter," Alex pointed out. His tone wasn't mean, just matter-of-fact. One cold hard raindrop struck him on his bare arm. Another struck him on the side of his nose.

"Don't stand under trees," Lizzie went on.

Dave, who had already taken shelter under the overhanging branches of a large fir tree, reluctantly returned to the trail.

"Don't lie down flat on the ground. Just crouch in place, preferably on your backpack, minimizing the area of your contact with the ground."

Alex was impressed. There was a reason why Lizzie was called "the Brain." How could she remember every word of her notes like that, verbatim? But remembering the instructions was one thing; carrying them out was another. How was Marcia supposed to crouch in place with a broken ankle? She'd just have to sit there, where the boys had placed her.

Lizzie and Dave were already pulling their rain ponchos out of their packs and then crouching as they were supposed to. Alex thought he had better try to find Marcia's lime green poncho: she was starting to shiver. He took it out of her pack and, as gently as he could, pulled it over Marcia's unprotesting head. He took his own poncho and spread it over her legs, like a blanket.

"What about you?" she asked.

"I'll be all right. I'm tough."

He grinned at her. Shakily, she smiled back.

Another flash of lightning, the brightest Alex had ever seen, rocked the sky. This time the thunder came simultaneously. So did the rain. The pelting raindrops were icy. They struck Alex's exposed arms like tiny bullets.

Alex felt the hairs on the back of his neck tingle. The next bolt of lightning struck. The thunder was so loud it was like being trapped inside a bass drum during the loudest, crashingest part of a symphony.

"Do you think we're going to die?" Lizzie asked in between lightning bolts. Her voice was small and strangled.

The same question had occurred to Alex.

Marcia sobbed. "If we die, it's all my fault. None of you would be out here now if it wasn't for me."

"It's not your fault," Alex snapped harshly. He knew all too well whose fault it was. "Lightning can strike you anywhere. It can strike you when you're at home sleeping in your own bed." Was that true? He didn't think it was. "It could be striking the rest of our group right now."

He thought for a second of his father. He couldn't

imagine his father being struck by lightning, or letting him, Alex, be struck by lightning if he was with him. He wondered if his father was worried about him now, or if he was just making sarcastic comments to the others about his fool son who didn't have sense enough to come in out of the rain. Alex would have gotten out of the rain if there had been anyplace to go. His shirt was soaking, wringing wet. He cradled his head in his hands.

"My hair," Marcia moaned. "I felt it in my hair."

Alex reached out and took hold of her hand. She held his so tightly that it would have hurt if it hadn't felt so good.

Then the rain started to ease up. The next lightning flash was farther away, the thunder delayed, more distant.

"It missed us," Alex said.

He was cold. He had never been colder in his life. The only part of him that wasn't frozen was the hand that Marcia was holding.

Dave touched his shoulder. "Do you have any other clothes? You'd better put on something dry."

He didn't want to let go of Marcia's hand, but he did. He peeled off his shirt and pulled on a sweatshirt. The dry, warm fabric felt good against his icy skin.

"Do you feel as if we had died, and now we're alive again, only more so, *more* alive than ever before?" Lizzie asked. She had helped Marcia take off her poncho and was stuffing it, and Alex's poncho, back into the two packs.

It was odd how Lizzie could put into words feelings that Alex hadn't even realized that he had. "Yeah," Alex said. "That's a good way of putting it. Ready, Barnett?"

Dave nodded.

"Madam, your chair awaits."

The three of them managed to get Marcia settled again.

"It can't be too much farther now," Alex said hopefully. "We're almost there."

Alex didn't know how much farther they had walked—*far*—or how much more time had gone by—*lots*—when finally—*finally*—he heard footsteps on the trail, coming toward them.

"Alex!" he heard someone calling. "Alex!"

The voice was his dad's.

Alex tried to yell back, but no sound came out. Dave shouted, and Lizzie joined in.

He was too tired to stop, too tired to think, too tired to do anything but continue putting one foot in front of the other, counting every step as he went.

Just twenty more steps.

Twenty more.

Twenty.

His dad came into sight, with one of the ranch guides beside him. "What the—" his dad began.

"She broke her ankle," Alex said wearily.

Then the ranch guide was there, lifting Marcia out of the boys' chair, setting her down on the trail, examining her bandaged ankle.

And for the first time in as long as he could remember, Alex was in his dad's arms, holding on tight to him, sobbing with exhaustion and relief.

12

LIZZIE WAS DOING ALL THE TALKING. Marcia lay on a couch in the cabin, waiting for the ranch truck to come to take her to the hospital. Alex and Dave were too tired to talk, too tired to do anything but sprawl on the floor and bask in everyone's admiration.

"So Marcia and I were resting, when we heard it, this dry *rattle* that sounded like it was about six feet away from us. I heard it first, but then Marcia heard it, too, and we knew it *had* to be a rattlesnake. What else could it be? What else is there in nature that *rattles*?"

This wasn't Alex's favorite part of the story. The rattle that had caused all the trouble was still in his pocket. He made a mental note to himself to chuck it into the bushes the next time he was outside with no one around.

"And then we heard this *rustling* kind of sound, or

maybe it was a *slithering* kind of sound. So: first the rattle, then the slither."

"And I screamed," Marcia put in. She looked pale, but the ranch guide had rebandaged her ankle and given her some ibuprofen to help with the pain and swelling. Alex thought that in a way she was enjoying herself, lying in state like an injured queen, all eyes upon her.

"And Marcia screamed, and I guess I screamed, too, and we started to run, the wrong way down the trail, but we wanted to get as far away from the rattlesnake as we could. Then there was a rock in the trail, and we didn't see it, and Marcia tripped and fell really hard. At first I thought—she lay there so quiet and still that I thought she was—but when I knelt down beside her I could see that she was still breathing. But then I saw her ankle, and it just looked terrible. I knew it had to be broken."

"*I* knew it was broken," Marcia said. "It hurt worse than anything ever hurt in my life. I think I even fainted for a while, you know, because of the pain."

Marcia was definitely looking pleased with herself now. Alex gathered that it was a high-status thing, for the girls, to faint.

"And *then*," Lizzie said, "Alex came." Her voice took on a new, warmer tone.

Across the room, Alex's dad flashed him a thumbs-up sign. His father then blew on an imaginary medal and shined it on his shirt. Alex knew that his father was pleased with him, genuinely, thoroughly pleased. *This* was the kind of story about his son that his dad liked people to hear.

"Alex came, with Dave, and he was *wonderful*. Right away he remembered all these things we had learned in first aid, about preventing shock, and everything."

Ms. Van Winkle interrupted the story. She, too, looked proud. "Didn't I tell you those first-aid skills could come in handy this week?" She beamed at Alex as if he had been her star student all along.

"So Alex found a splint," Lizzie went on. "He just searched until he found some sticks that would do. And he bandaged Marcia's ankle with a couple of bandannas."

The ranch guide had used official gauze bandages when he attended to Marcia's ankle. Alex saw that Marcia was clutching the bandanna in her right hand, like a comfort object. All alleged cracks about it were forgiven and forgotten now.

"We didn't know if we should try to walk on to the cabins, or if we should wait for help, but Alex didn't think help would come soon enough, so he and Dave *carried* Marcia—carried her *every step of the way*."

Well, not every step. The last half mile or so, the ranch guide and Alex's dad had taken turns carrying her. But Alex and Dave had carried her far enough that Alex knew his muscles would ache from it tomorrow.

"Son," the ranch guide said, turning toward Alex as he spoke, "all I can say is that it was a lucky thing for this young lady that you happened to be so close at hand when the accident happened. Boys and girls, teachers, parents, I think this young man deserves a round of applause."

Then they were all clapping, the boys whistling and stamping for good measure.

"Dave carried her, too," Alex added, uncomfortable for once at all the attention directed his way.

"Let's hear another round of applause for Dave, and for you too, miss." The ranch guide nodded toward Lizzie. "I'm sure you were a big comfort to your friend along the way. And you, our little wounded gal. You were plenty brave. Folks, let's give 'em all a hand."

More applause.

"And now," Ms. Van Winkle called out, "if we're going to have any chow tonight, I need sixth-period family living in the kitchen to get things started."

Ms. Van Winkle had organized the menu so that each class would help with one stage of the food preparation. Alex was in the sixth-period class, so he hoisted himself off the floor and got ready to follow the others into the kitchen.

"You've done enough, Alex," Ms. Van Winkle told him. "Just take it easy for a while."

Alex gladly reclined on one of the couches vacated by some of the sixth-period family living chefs. It was the couch right next to Marcia's. He wondered if she would speak to him, now that the chaos had subsided and most of the other kids had gone. Alex's dad had drifted out to the front porch with some of the other parents.

Alex, I don't know how I can ever thank you.

Aw, it was nothing.

She didn't say a word.

Maybe he needed to feed her a cue. "You doing okay?" he asked. "The truck'll be here any minute, I think, to take you to the hospital." Marcia's parents had been called, and they were on their way from West Creek, too.

"I wish it were all over."

"It will be."

"I'll have to have a cast all summer long, and I won't be able to go swimming at the pool. And I'm on the West Creek tennis team, too. Or I *was*."

Alex didn't blame her for moping. He felt another pang of guilt as he thought of how differently the day would have turned out if he had left his snake rattle at home. But if he had, Marcia wouldn't be chatting with him, either. Not that he would ever have hurt her deliberately just to get her to talk to him.

"I'm glad I was there when it happened," he said. It occurred to him that so far no one had questioned why he was there when it happened. Perhaps it was better not to call attention to the odd coincidence.

Marcia didn't miss her cue this time. "I'm glad

you were there, too," she said softly. "Thanks, Alex."

He flashed her his friendliest grin. "Anytime," he said.

"Marcia, our ride is here," Mrs. Martin called. Mrs. Martin was going with Marcia to the emergency room, to stay with her until her parents arrived.

The ranch guide and another dad appeared to carry Marcia to the truck.

"Good luck," Alex called after her, the friendly grin fading from his face. In his last glimpse of her, Marcia looked small and scared, her face white again with pain as her ankle was inevitably jostled. The truth was that Marcia *would* have a cast on her ankle for weeks, she *would* miss swimming and tennis, and it was all Alex's fault.

Alex lay back weakly on the couch. He was so hungry he almost felt sick to his stomach. Or was it the guilt about his unconfessed role in the accident that was making his stomach churn?

It wasn't as if he had done anything *that* terrible, Alex reasoned. The terrible consequences were as much Marcia's fault as his own. Just because you thought you heard a rattlesnake didn't mean you had to run down the trail like an idiot and not look where you were going and trip and break your ankle. All the same, even though he hadn't planned for any of this to happen, none of it would have happened if it hadn't been for his plan.

The ranch guide returned. He plunked himself down on the arm of Alex's couch. Alex hoped he wasn't going to make another speech about what a big hero Alex had been.

"Poor little thing," the guide said, obviously referring to Marcia.

Alex remembered that the guide's name was Sam. Sam sighed, as if doubtful that Marcia would live through the truck ride to the hospital. Alex could imagine that it wouldn't be all that comfortable riding in the back of a truck for twenty miles on bumpy, rutted dirt roads.

"We've had broken bones before," Sam said. "And a concussion—no, make that two concussions. Hypothermia—I'm surprised you folks didn't get it today, out there in the rain, with insufficient rain gear. Insect bites. Poison ivy. Yup. We've seen it all, just about."

The memory of past calamities seemed to cheer Sam. Maybe he enjoyed playing the role of hero, too.

"Not snakebite, though. We've never had a case of snakebite. Not in the six years I've been working here. We go ahead and warn folks about snakes—standard procedure, warn 'em about everything. But I think this is our first report of a snake encounter, especially at this altitude and on an overcast day. Those critters usually lay low and don't rattle unless someone disturbs them sunbathing on a rock."

Alex squirmed. His stomach squirmed with him.

"Let me ask you something, son. You think these girls really heard a snake? Seems unlikely to me. You know how kids are. Girls especially." He winked at Alex; Alex didn't wink back. "You think it was all in their minds, like? Something they talked themselves into thinking they heard?"

"I don't know," Alex said uncomfortably. "Maybe." But he didn't want Sam thinking Marcia and Lizzie were hysterical, either. "Lizzie is pretty reliable." That made it sound as if Marcia wasn't. But Sam wasn't going to see any of them again, after tomorrow, so it didn't much matter what he thought.

Alex's father appeared and perched on the other arm of the couch. He looked down at Alex, his face beaming with fatherly satisfaction, even though his smile was still slightly mocking.

"Feeling better?"

It was too much, to be trapped between his father on one arm of the sofa and Sam on the other.

"Actually," Alex said, "my stomach doesn't feel so hot." His stomach was back on the bus again, lurching over the twisting switchbacks of the mountain pass.

He was going to be sick. He got up unsteadily from the couch and staggered toward the door and threw up in the dirty snow bank beside the porch.

Before stumbling inside again, he remembered to hurl his snake rattle as far as he could into the twilight.

13

THE NEXT MORNING, THE THIRD-PERIOD family-living class made pancakes; the second-period family-living class made scrambled eggs and sausage cakes; the fourth-period family-living class prepared a fruit platter. It all looked surprisingly good, but Alex's stomach still wasn't ready for it. He ate half a pancake, then pushed his plate away.

Dazzling blue skies greeted them when they stepped out of the cabins for the hike back.

"Don't forget sunscreen," Ms. S. reminded the clump of kids standing near Alex.

Alex found his bottle of sunscreen in his pack. Unfortunately, he hadn't put the cap back on tightly enough the last time he used it, and the bottle was sticky with spilled sunscreen. So was the balled-up, still clammy T-shirt that he had stuck in there yesterday after the storm and forgotten to take out again. The whole thing was pretty disgusting. Alex smeared some sunscreen on, stuck the bottle back in his pack, and zipped it shut again.

As the seventh grade started hiking, Dave fell into step beside Alex. Alex was relieved to have Dave as his partner again: with Dave he didn't have to keep on pretending to be a hero. But he hoped Dave wasn't going to be asking him for any more plans. Alex was finished with plans for the rest of his life.

"Man, my legs are sore," Dave began. "And my shoulders. And my arms."

"Yeah," Alex said. "Mine, too."

They walked for a while in silence. That was the best thing about being a guy, Alex thought: you could walk along with somebody and not have to be yakking all the time. Up ahead, he saw Lizzie yakking with Alison. Was she still yakking about him? He hoped not.

In his head Alex heard Sam-the-ranch-guide's voice: "All I can say is that it was a lucky thing for this young lady that you happened to be so close at hand when the accident happened." He saw his dad, hovering protectively by him, that proud look in his eyes, asking, "Feeling better?"

He wasn't feeling better. If anything, he was feeling even worse.

"It wasn't really our fault," Dave said, out of the blue.

Alex just looked at him. The denial, which had seemed plausible enough yesterday when Alex had made it to himself, sounded thoroughly pathetic when said aloud.

"Well, not a hundred percent our fault," Dave amended.

"Ninety-eight?" Alex asked.

"No more than ninety." Dave flashed him a grin. Then he turned serious again. "You're not going to say anything." The statement was clearly a question.

"No." What would be the point? What was done was done. A big dramatic confession wouldn't miraculously heal Marcia's broken bone. And if he spoke up now, everyone would wonder why he hadn't said anything before, when Lizzie was telling her story, when Sam was leading the others in applause. If he spoke up now, he'd just make himself—and everybody else—look ridiculous.

Because the hike back to the lodge was mostly downhill, unlike the hike up to the cabins, they made much better time and reached the lodge picnic area by mid-afternoon.

"Free time until dinner," Coach Krubek announced. "We'll eat at five-thirty."

"Nature journals!" Ms. S. sang out. "We'll be sharing from our journals in our program tonight."

Alex wasn't going to be sharing anything from *his*

nature journal, that was for sure. Its pages were completely blank, except for his rain poem, which he didn't feel like reading to anyone now.

Then he remembered: hadn't Ms. S. said that their nature journals were worth 10 percent of their English grade for the trimester? Wearily, Alex fished his journal from his backpack. It, too, was covered with spilled sunscreen.

"You're kidding," Dave said when he saw what Alex was doing.

"It's part of our grade," Alex said. "I have to write *something*."

"I'm getting a C in English already," Dave said. "See ya later."

Alex sat himself at a picnic table, wiped sunscreen off his pencil, and started writing. He remembered a lot of things he had seen on the hike. Juniper bushes. Pine trees. Tiny darting chipmunks. One lone circling hawk. He was pretty good at drawing, so he made a picture of the hawk on one page.

When he glanced up from his drawing, he saw Ms. S. standing a few feet away, watching him. "Write about your experiences yesterday," she suggested in her low, gentle voice. "It was a wonderful story when Lizzie told it last night. I'd love to hear your version in your journal. You could read it to all of us this evening during our sharing time."

Alex gave a noncommittal smile; Ms. S. walked away. He could just imagine the journal entry he would write about his heroic rescue of Marcia:

So Marcia had been giving me the cold shoulder, see? So I decided to play a trick on her. I had this rattlesnake rattle that I had brought to camp just to cause trouble for somebody, and so I hid behind some bushes and rattled it, and made this rustling sound. And the rest is history.

Yeah. Right. He was going to share that with the group tonight?

Alex wrote a paragraph describing the lightning storm and then closed his journal and put it back in his pack, which now reeked of sunscreen. If Lizzie read aloud from her journal, that should take up the whole sharing time, sparing everybody else.

Sometimes, Alex was learning, silence was best.

Alex tuned out during most of the evening program. There were lots of descriptions of trees and birds and clouds and rain. Lizzie's were definitely the most poetic. Ms. S. looked at him inquiringly the first time she called for volunteers. He gave a slight shake of his head, and after that she left him alone.

Friday morning they went on a shorter hike to see some Indian ruins. The ruins looked like a bunch of broken bricks to Alex. Mesa Verde this wasn't. Mrs. Martin, back from the hospital, led the tour. But first she answered some questions about Marcia.

"Her right ankle is broken," Mrs. Martin said. "The doctor said it was a clean break, broken in just one place, and should heal well. They put on a cast and gave her a pair of crutches, which she'll need for about six weeks."

That didn't sound too bad. Six weeks wasn't *that* long. It would leave Marcia the second half of the summer for her swimming and tennis. And everybody would make a big fuss over her at school, when she hobbled in on her crutches. Alex knew Marcia would see to that.

After the hike, they returned to the picnic area and ate the box lunches provided by the ranch. As soon as Alex sat down at his table, other kids flocked to join him. Dave, of course, and Ethan and Julius. Even some of the girls. Marcia's friend Sarah made a point of stopping by to tell him how wonderful he was: "I just want to say that I think it's, like, great, what you did for Marcia." Tall Tanya, Alex noted with alarm, had taken to gazing at him with adoring eyes.

Alex had a feeling that if there were another square dance right now, he wouldn't be partners with Mrs. Martin. The girls would be lining up to dance with him. Even Marcia.

Except that, in the hospital with a broken ankle, Marcia couldn't dance.

The bus ride home was as bumpy and curvy as the bus ride to the ranch, but Alex managed to sleep most of the way. When he staggered off the bus back in West Creek, queasy and stiff-legged, his mother was there to greet them. She gave Alex a long, tight hug and then turned to kiss his dad.

"The house was so quiet without you two!" she exclaimed. "Cara and I were going crazy, listening to ourselves rattle around in it."

"Where was Dax?" Alex's dad asked. "Was he rattling, too?"

Rattling. Alex cringed. His mom ignored the question, instead giving Alex another hug. Something about the hug—the sense that his mother had really, truly missed him, that she really, truly loved him *no matter what*—made Alex fight with himself to hold back tears.

"So," she said when she finally released him, "how was it? Tell me all about it. I want to hear everything."

"Good!" his dad said. "Because we have some stories to tell."

Always one to seek maximum dramatic effect, his dad didn't launch into the big story in the car. He told about the mountain biking: "I may be pushing fifty, but let me tell you, none of those kids were passing me on the trails." He told about the ranch's great barbecue the first night: "I hate to say it, hon, but you have some competition in the cooking department."

Alex was relieved that he *didn't* tell about the square dancing: *And when the girls had finished picking their partners, guess who was left over? Yup, you guessed it. Our son, Alex.*

When they reached home, Cara's car was parked in front of the house. "Is Lover Boy here, too?" Alex's dad asked, not seeming to expect an answer.

Both Cara and Dax were in the kitchen, eating a snack. Cara, not usually one for hugging, got up to give Alex a quick squeeze. Dax raised his hand in greeting. He was wearing the diamond stud. Alex saw his dad's eyes go to it, too.

"You survived," Cara said.

"Barely," his dad said, settling himself into a kitchen chair. He was obviously ready to tell the story now. Alex had the sense that he didn't even mind Dax's being there. The bigger the audience, the better.

"Uh-oh," his mother said. "Is this something I want to hear?"

"You bet it is."

Alex's dad told the story, pretty much the way Lizzie had told it. He threw in an impersonation of Marcia, squealing as she ran away from the "snake." He made a bit more of Lizzie's thinking Marcia might be dead. He gave more fanfare to Alex's heroic arrival upon the scene.

His dad was a great storyteller. None of the others seemed to think it odd that his dad was telling Alex's story, not Alex. They were used to listening to his dad talk. Alex wouldn't have wanted to tell the story, anyway. It was a big enough lie just to listen to it. It would have been a monstrous lie to tell his dad's version of it himself, in his own words.

He felt his mother's eyes on him, filled with pride. That was how she always looked at both her children. Cara seemed impressed in spite of herself, as if she hadn't suspected that her kid brother had it in him. Dax gave Alex an approving smile, but there was a question in his eyes. There was no way he could have known the truth. Maybe he was puzzled by Alex's unsmiling silence during the telling of his triumph.

"You two must be starving," Alex's mother said when the story was finished. "I hope so; I made a cake."

Alex ate a thick wedge of it while his dad went upstairs to check his e-mail and his mom went downstairs to check the laundry.

"You're not into it, the whole hero thing," Dax observed.

Alex *would* have been "into" it, if he had really been a hero. "Well, it's just—I mean—I really wasn't a hero.

It really didn't happen—completely—the way Dad said."

Maybe he had already revealed too much.

Cara laughed. "When has anything ever happened completely the way Dad said?"

"It's not just Dad. It's everybody. Saying this. Saying that. I guess I'm just tired of hearing it, that's all. It's like—just because they *think* something is one way doesn't mean it *is* that way."

"Remember Thoreau?" Dax asked.

"Sort of."

" 'What a man thinks of himself, that it is which determines, or rather, indicates, his fate.' "

Alex carried his empty plate to the dishwasher. That was the whole problem, right there. His dad, his mom, his sister, his teachers, Sam-the-ranch-guide, Marcia, his friends—with the exception of Dave, they all thought he was a hero. In the opinion of the rest of the world, he was doing great. He was the only person who had a low opinion of himself right now. But if Dax and Thoreau were right, his was the only opinion that counted.

His father looked up from the computer, seeming surprised at the sight of Alex, positioned in the door to the home office. "Two hundred and fourteen e-mails," Alex's dad said. "And I even checked my e-mail from my laptop at the ranch this morning."

"Dad." Alex didn't know if he could get the words out. "Do you remember the real rattlesnake rattle Grandpa gave me that time?"

"Sure. What of it?"

"Well, the rattle Marcia and Lizzie heard on the trail—"

Alex didn't have to finish his sentence. His dad gave a hearty guffaw. "I should have figured it out. That guide Sam kept saying that they'd never had an encounter with snakes on the trail before. My son, the hero! Oh, this is a good one!"

His dad didn't look angry. Alex knew this was the kind of prank his dad could have pulled when he was young.

"I have to say something. I mean, to somebody."

Alex's dad's face changed.

"I mean, I can't take it anymore, everybody going on and on about it when it was all my fault in the first place."

"You're joking, aren't you?" His dad's voice was harsh and critical now. "Are you crazy? If you thought yakking about that broken tree branch would cause trouble, what about some kid's broken bone? You want her dad suing me for all their hospital bills? Use your head, Alex. Right now you have it both ways. You had your fun, and you got to be hailed as a hero afterward. It sounds pretty good to me."

"But it's all a lie," Alex said desperately.

"Look. Half of what I do as a lawyer is to lie. No, not to *lie*, exactly, but to be selective about what truths I tell, and when and where, and to whom. Let this die down of its own accord. You blow the lid open on this thing, Alex, and you'll be the laughingstock of your school, and your mother and I will be the laughing-stock of the PTO. There is a time for talking, the Good Book says, and a time for keeping your mouth shut. This is a time for keeping your mouth shut."

There was so much else that Alex wanted to say, that he needed to say. Not now, and not to his dad. But someday, to somebody. He didn't know how he'd tell the truth—could he really walk up to Marcia and just *say* it?—but he knew he'd tell it somehow. He didn't have to act the way his dad acted. He didn't have to do the things his dad would do. In the end it didn't matter what his dad thought of him, or said about him, to his friends, to his coach, even to the whole school. What mattered was what Alex thought of himself.

His dad looked at him, hard. Then he winked, as if to show Alex that he wasn't really mad. And he turned back to his two hundred and fourteen e-mails.

14

ALEX TOOK THE LAST SEAT in the back row of the multi-purpose room. Of course, his father sat in the center of the front row, this time with Alex's mom beside him. At least tonight his dad wasn't going to make any embarrassing speeches. Parents didn't get a chance to speak at the end-of-year awards program. They just sat and clapped as their children paraded up to accept various awards. This year the seventh-grade program was held on Wednesday evening, the week after outdoor ed.

Marcia came in with Sarah; she sat on the aisle and laid her crutches on the floor beside her. Even though, as Alex had predicted, Marcia was making the most of her crutches as an attention-getting device, he still had a pang every time he saw them. Marcia's broken ankle was *real*. It wasn't something she had dreamed up to make Alex feel guilty for playing his prank on her. The broken branch on Marcia's tree was real, too. And, in a way, Marcia's hurt feelings after his zit remark had been the most real of all. All the confessions and apologies that he still hadn't found the right time and place to make smoldered inside him.

Dave sank into the seat next to Alex. Alex couldn't imagine that Dave would get any awards at all, the way he goofed off in school. Maybe he'd get a perfect attendance award, or something. Dave was there all the time to help Alex carry out his plans. But Alex was through with plans for good—at least plans that broke any bones, or tree branches, or hearts.

Alex knew that he himself was going to get an award for being on the Principal's List, the list of kids with all A's and B's on their report card. It was a pretty long list, but if you had even one C you couldn't be on it. Alex also expected to get an award for general excellence in math. Probably twenty kids would get that one. Still, it was something for his dad and mom to clap about.

The multipurpose room was practically full. Alex saw Ethan and Julius, Alison and Lizzie, and tall Tanya, who no longer blushed and giggled whenever she passed Alex in the hall. It was a good thing that feelings faded from lack of encouragement.

Dr. Stanley spoke into the microphone. "Good

evening, West Creek parents and students." This time there were no problems with the mike. "It's my great pleasure to welcome you all to the seventh-grade end-of-year awards program," he began.

"It's his great pleasure that the school year is almost over," Alex whispered to Dave.

"Ours, too," Dave whispered back to Alex.

"Our first award goes to students who have had perfect attendance throughout the school year. Six students are receiving this award. Students, please stand when your names are called. Parents, please hold your applause until all the names have been read. David Barnett, Amy Daniels . . ."

Dave stood in place, hamming up his joy at receiving the first award of the evening. Alex had to yank him back down again when the principal went on to the next award.

The program was long and dull. Half the awards, it seemed, went to Lizzie. She had scored the most points for the Mathletes, the new school math team; her poem was chosen as the best one in the West Creek literary magazine, *Creek Dreams*; a paper she had written for social studies had won some statewide essay contest. In between Lizzie's awards, other kids got an award or two: an award for Lizzie, an award for someone else, an award for Lizzie, an award for someone else.

Alex caught a glimpse of his mother's proud smile

and his father's half-mocking grin as he collected his own three awards: the two he had predicted, plus another for being one of the three top medalists on the West Creek track-and-field team. It was funny: when it came to running, Alex didn't even care whether or not he got an award. All he cared about was the running itself.

Ethan was handed a certificate for taking second place in the science fair, back in February; Julius got some community service award for starting a babysitting program for parents during West Creek sporting events; Lizzie's friend Alison had won a piano competition; Marcia was recognized for having been on the tennis team. Her awkward limping to the podium on her crutches drew the biggest applause of the evening. Alex clapped hard for her, too.

"I now have one last award of special merit to present," Dr. Stanley said, just as Alex thought the program would never end and he would spend the rest of his life trapped in the multipurpose room watching Lizzie Archer get an award for everything. "We've recognized academic excellence in every subject area, excellence in sports, excellence in the arts, excellence in community service, even excellence in attendance."

At the mention of the word "attendance," Dave began his pantomime of preening again. Alex thought he'd have to stop him from rising to his feet for a second bow.

"There is one other form of excellence we should honor tonight. It may sound old-fashioned, but there is a form of excellence we can sum up in the simple word *hero*."

Alex felt his stomach begin to churn. More than anything, he hoped Dr. Stanley wasn't talking about his "rescue" of Marcia at outdoor ed. He tried to remember what else had happened during the whole year that could be called heroic. He came up with a blank.

"The person I am calling a hero tonight," Dr. Stanley went on after the rustle of speculation running through the audience had died down, "had to think quickly in an emergency situation. He had to use the first-aid skills learned in his family-living class and apply them in a real-life situation."

Everyone was turning around to look at Alex now. He felt like running out of the room before Dr. Stanley could finish. He felt like throwing up on the floor.

"This person had to make decisions under pressure, decisions that would affect others' lives as well as his own. And he and his companion had to bear the burden of carrying one of his classmates to safety."

Dr. Stanley paused again, for effect. He was only making it worse by dragging out the announcement.

"You know who I'm talking about, don't you?" Dr.

Stanley asked, smiling down at the assembled seventh graders.

For answer, they began to chant: "Al-ex. Al-ex. Al-ex."

"Please come up here," Dr. Stanley said. "Alex Ryan."

Somehow Alex made his way to the podium. Dr. Stanley shook his hand and drew him in front of the mike, lowering it so that Alex could speak into it easily. No one else that evening had been invited to give an acceptance speech for an award.

What if he accepted the award, just took it and walked away, and vowed never to let himself get into such a mess ever again? No. If he didn't say now, for once and for all, what needed to be said, he would hate himself for the rest of his life.

To keep himself from looking out at the audience, he fastened his eyes on the ceiling. He didn't want to see his father's face.

"I—I can't accept this award," he said.

Dr. Stanley leaned down toward the mike. "Son, every true hero thinks that what he did was nothing. But the award is yours. You earned it."

"No I didn't." Alex's voice came out stronger now.

Dr. Stanley, as if aware that the award presentation wasn't going as planned, put his arm around Alex's shoulder to draw him from the podium and send him back to his seat.

Alex broke away from him. "Marcia ran down the trail because she heard a rattlesnake," he said into the mike. "I was the rattlesnake. That was me. I had a snake rattle with me, and I rattled it, just to scare her and make her scream. I didn't mean for anything bad to happen. I never meant for her to get hurt."

The multipurpose room was deadly quiet now. Alex stared at his feet. There. They could all hate him again. They could laugh at him, pick him last for square dancing, he didn't care. No, he *did* care. But there was something else he cared about even more. He cared about being able to live with himself.

Alex started back to his seat. The shocked silence in the large room continued unbroken. Alex felt a stab of pity for Dr. Stanley. He hadn't expected the festive awards assembly to end this way.

The principal finally cleared his throat. "Making a mistake and being big enough to admit it," Dr. Stanley said. "In my book, that's heroism, too."

Alex reached his seat just as Dave jumped to his feet and began clapping. Then the others—parents and teachers, and Dr. Stanley himself—joined in.

"Now please join us for a wonderful reception next door in the cafeteria, provided for us by the PTO," Dr. Stanley said.

Alex had never heard anyone sound more relieved. The seventh-grade end-of-year awards assembly was over.

Kids sitting near Alex held up their hands to him for high fives. In a trance, Alex returned them.

"Man, that took guts," Dave said. "I have no guts. I'm a gutless wonder."

Ethan shook Alex's hand. Julius pounded Alex on the back. Across the room he caught a glimpse of his parents, trying to make their way toward him, held back by the mob of kids surrounding him.

Alex didn't wait for them. He pushed through the other kids till he reached Marcia; she couldn't leave her seat until the crowd had thinned, so she wouldn't get knocked over on her crutches.

"You were right all along," Alex said, before she could say anything. "You were right to hate me."

Marcia looked up at him. He couldn't tell if she was going to smile, or if she was going to cry. "I don't hate you," she said in a half-whisper. "I never hated you. Well, not a *lot*."

A good-looking, broad-shouldered, almost completely bald man appeared behind Marcia, holding hands with an attractive platinum blonde. Marcia's parents.

Alex was not looking forward to what was going to come next. Would he have to pay for all of Marcia's medical bills? What else could the law do to a kid who caused another kid to have a serious accident? He was too young to go to jail. He guessed they could make him do hundreds and hundreds of hours of community service. He had visions of helping Julius babysit at every school event from now until he graduated from high school.

Mr. Faitak looked him over. Alex recognized the look. It was a tactic of intimidation favored by his own father. Its name was "Let 'Em Squirm."

"So," Mr. Faitak said with no hint of amusement in his voice, "you were the rattlesnake."

Alex met his eyes. "I was the rattlesnake."

"I don't suppose that you were also the toilet-paper artist who paid us a visit some weeks ago?"

"I was the toilet-paper artist." At least *artist* had a nice ring to it. "And, sir, I'm sorry about the tree branch, really I am. And about Marcia's ankle, too. Even sorrier. Much sorrier."

"This gives me the chance to ask something I've always wanted to ask one of these T.P. artists," Mr. Faitak said.

"Yes, sir?"

"*Why?*"

"Why, sir?"

"Why would someone spend all that time and effort doing something so pointless? It *is* pointless, isn't it? There is no *point* to it at all, is there?" Mr. Faitak sounded as scornful as Alex's father.

Alex knew he might regret what he was going to say next even more than everything else that had happened so far, but he had to say it anyway. "Um—the point? The point is—um—to show some girl that you like her."

He forced himself to look at Marcia. Her face was flushed with happiness. He quickly looked away. But what he had said was true. He *did* like Marcia. And he wanted her to like him.

"Well, that clears things up considerably," Mr. Faitak said, his face a tad less grim. "So what happens now? What kind of restitution are you prepared to make?"

Was this where Alex was supposed to offer to pay the tree man and the ankle doctor? He knew he should pay *something*. He *wanted* to pay something.

"Um—whatever you say, sir."

"Well, since you're so fond of our tree, you can come over this fall and rake its leaves. And while you're at it, we have another twenty trees on our property, all great ones for producing colorful fall foliage."

Alex waited to see if Mr. Faitak was going to add anything else to his "sentence," but he seemed to be finished. "All right, sir. I'll do that, sir," Alex said quickly. He saw himself toiling away as Marcia and her girlfriends lolled in lawn chairs, sipping hot spiced cider and giggling at every stroke of his rake. But he had expected far worse and couldn't say that he deserved any better.

Mr. Faitak helped Marcia onto her crutches and led the way to the reception. Alex would have felt limp with relief, except for one thing. He still had to face his father.

Alex spotted him as soon as he walked into the reception. His father was standing in a group of other dads, holding forth on some topic. Kids today, and how dumb they were compared to kids long ago? School policy on field trips, and how it could be improved if only teachers would have the sense to listen to him?

His mother was waiting for Alex. Without a word, she drew him into one of her great hugs. Alex didn't resist it. He let her hug him, and he hugged her back.

"I'm proud of you," she said. "Not just for your awards, but for what you said into the mike just now. All of us do things we're sorry for all the time. What matters is what we do afterward to try to make things right again."

Well, Alex was also planning to do fewer things in the future that he'd have to be sorry for.

His dad looked in his direction and slowly started walking toward him. This was it.

"You had to do it your way, didn't you," his dad said once the obligatory "Let 'Em Squirm" moment had passed. "I'm surprised you didn't arrange to make your confession on national television. 'My name is Alex Ryan, and I'm a no-good skunk.' " He let a fake sob creep into his voice.

"Al." Alex's mother laid a warning hand on his arm.

"No," he said. "It's fine. It worked. You're a bigger hero than ever. All the other dads are pumping my hand in congratulations for my part in raising you."

Alex looked away. "That's not the point," he muttered.

"No? And what, may I ask, is the point?" This conversation was beginning to sound like a replay of the one with Marcia's father.

"Dax says— Well, Dax says that Thoreau says that what matters isn't what other people think, but what *you* think. About yourself."

" '*Dax* says,' " his father repeated. " '*Dax* says.' It's a dark day when my son takes his cues from the Daxes of this world. Next you'll be getting a little rosebud earring, I expect."

Alex gave up. He should have known better than to mention Dax to his father.

"Come on, you two," Alex's mom said pleadingly. "Let's eat."

His dad turned away. His dad didn't understand. He would never understand. But right then it was enough for Alex that he had done what *he* thought was right. Alex couldn't change his father; it was useless to try. But at least Alex had taken one small step toward changing himself.

"I hope some of your cake is left," he told his mom.

She smiled at him, tears in her eyes.

"Alex!" Marcia called to him from the refreshment table, holding her fork upright like a queen's scepter. Alex obeyed her summons.

"I saved a piece of cake for you," she said, leaning on her crutches, gazing at him with her big, blue eyes.

It wasn't his mother's rich, dark, homemade chocolate cake but a dry, powdery, store-bought cake, covered with bright pink, sticky, gooey, too-sweet icing.

Alex savored every bite.